Amanda M. [

In Wild Rose Time

Amanda M. Douglas

In Wild Rose Time

1st Edition | ISBN: 978-3-75232-909-4

Place of Publication: Frankfurt am Main, Germany

Year of Publication: 2020

Outlook Verlag GmbH, Germany.

IN WILD ROSE TIME

BY

AMANDA M. DOUGLAS

I—A HANDFUL OF ROSES

"Hev a bunch o' roses, mem? Fresh wild roses with the dew on 'em. Jes' picked. On'y ten cents."

They dropped in at the open window, and landed on Virginia Deering's lap. Her first impulse was to throw them out again, as she half said to herself, "I hate wild roses, I always shall!" But she glanced down into such a forlorn, wistful face, that her heart was touched, a not unkindly heart, though it had been bitter and obdurate with the unreason of youth.

"Oh, please buy 'em, mem. Mammy's sick and can't do nothin', an' Ben's got a fever. On'y ten cents."

The poor child, in her ragged dress, was clean enough. Her face had a starved, eager look, and the earnest pleading in the eyes bespoke necessity seldom counterfeited. Miss Deering opened her pretty silver-clasped purse and handed out a quarter.

"All of it?" hesitatingly. "Oh, thanky, thanky! We'd sold the chickens, and everything we could, and Ben said city folks was fond of wild-flowers."

The whistle blew. There was a groan and quiver as the train began to move, that drowned the child's gratitude. Miss Deering laid the roses on the seat beside her with a curious touch, as if she shrank from them. An hour or two ago she had started on her journey, leaving behind her a sweet dream of youth and love and roses. In twenty-four hours the brightness of her life had been swept away. The summer day wore a dulness she had never seen before.

She was a handsome young girl, with a fine complexion, light, silken soft hair, and very dark gray eyes. A modern, stylish girl, who had not yet reached the period when one begins to assert her right supreme over the world and all that therein is.

She peered at the newcomers at the next station. No one wanted the seat, however. The sweet wild roses, in all their shell-like transparency, lay unheeded, drinking up the dewy crystal drops that had been showered by mortal hands, as well as dusky-fingered night. You would have said she had a tender side, that could be keenly moved by beauty. Perhaps that was why she glanced out of the window on the whirling sights. She might have vaguely wondered if she had been so utterly right yesterday—was it yesterday, or a month ago?

She took up her book, but it had lost its interest. The delicate fragrance of the roses disturbed her—stirred a gust of feeling that she had fancied securely laid. If *he* had cared, he would have come last night; he would have seen her this morning at the station. She had felt so strong, so justified in her own sight, and such a simple thing as a beggar with wild roses had disturbed it all.

There were not many people coming in town. She glanced about—one and another had bunches of flowers, flaunting scarlet geraniums and modern things. Very few people cared for wild roses, unless they were worked in table-scarfs or painted on china. Ah, how the tender little buds crept closer to each other! The pink, shell-like leaves of the mothers drooped tiredly, the soft green huddled about with a kind of frightened tenderness, as if they might be going out in a strange, unfriendly world. She turned her eyes away with a betraying mistiness in them.

They came into the great station, but this was not the hour for crowds. She picked up her satchel, her book—should she leave the roses to the mercy of the sweeper? Something throbbed up in her throat, she gathered them with a desperate grasp, threaded her way through the great enclosure, and passed out into the street amid a babel of voices.

A group of ragged urchins stood eager for a chance to seize a valise or parcel, to the relief or disgust of its owner.

"Who wants some flowers?" bethinking herself suddenly of the flower charities.

They thronged round her. She threw the bunch with a light effort just beyond the first noisy ring. A shock-headed lad with a broad, freckled face and laughing blue eyes caught it. Another snatched at it. Thereupon ensued a scrimmage. Blows and tearing of hair were the courtesies exchanged, until a policeman loomed in sight. The first lad was at this moment the victor, and he plunged down the side street with a fleetness known only to the street arab. The majesty of the law distributed cuffs liberally among the vanquished, and the rabble dispersed.

Miss Deering smiled with a touch of sad scorn, nodded to a cabman, and, as she seated herself, watched the fleet but dirty feet vanishing in the distance, recalling the face.

"It's curious they, too, should quarrel about wild roses," she said, just under her breath, sighing softly.

Meanwhile Patsey Muldoon ran some ten or twelve squares, then paused for a bit of breath, mopping his face with his ragged shirt sleeve.

"My, ain't they queer? not stunners exactly, but splendid, if they ain't red. I d'know as Dil ever see sich a swad in her life. An' Bess's blue eyes'll be like saucers. Oh, golly! how sweet!" burying his face in them. "Sich as these ain't layin' loose round Barker's Court offen. I've lost a job mebbe, an' Casey'll crow if he gits one; but that ere left-hander wos science, that wos!" and the boy chuckled as he ran on again.

From the Grand Central over to the East Side tenements was no mean stretch, but Patsey would have gone twice as far to give Dilsey Quinn a pleasure.

The street was built up compactly, and swarmed with children. There was an open way between a row of houses, a flagged space called Barker's Court; a deep strip of ground that had been a puzzle to its owner, until he hit upon a plan for his model tenement row. The four-story houses faced each other, with pulley-lines between, the clothes shutting out air and light. They were planned for the greatest number, if the greatest good had been omitted. One narrow hall and stairway did for two houses, so not much space was lost. But the sights and sounds, the piles of garbage, the vile air emanating from rooms where dirt reigned supreme, and the steam of the wet clothes, were something terrible on a hot summer day. The poor creatures crowded into it were used to it.

Patsey ran down to the middle of the Court, and then scudded up one flight.

The room was clean, rather cheery looking, with one window, water and drain in the corner, a room at the back, and a very small one at the side over the hall, with a window half the width of the other. A stove stood in the chimney recess, there was an old lounge, a rug of crazy-work carpet in which Dilsey Quinn had sewed together the bits given to her mother.

"Hello, Dil! Ain't them the daisies? Did ye ever have sich a lot before in yer life? I don't mean they're reg'lar daisies—they're roses of some kind, but blam'd if I ever seen any like 'em afore."

He tossed them into a baby-wagon, where sat the frailest and whitest wraith one could ever imagine alive. How she lived puzzled everybody. They never took into account Dil's passionate and inexhaustible love that fought off death with eager, watchful care.

"O Patsey!" Such a joyful cry of surprise. "Was there a flower mission?"

"Flower mission be blowed! Did ye ever see any sich in a mission by the time it gits round here?"

His stubby nose wrinkled disdainfully, and he gave his head an important toss.

"But, oh, where *did* you get thim?" There was the least bit of a brogue in Dil's voice, and she always said "thim" in an odd, precise fashion. "There must be a thousand; they're packed so tight they've almost hurted each other. And, oh, how sweet!"

The breath of fragrance seemed to penetrate every pulse in Dil's sturdy frame.

"I guess ther ain't mor'n a hundred; but it's a jolly lot, and they looked so strange and queer like—weakly, like Bess here, an' I thought of her. A young lady throwed 'em out to me. I s'pose she'd had so many flowers they didn't count. My, wasn't she a high-stepper, purty as they make 'em; but her hair couldn't shine along o' Bess's here. None o' yer horse-car folks, nuther; she went off in a cab. An' Jim Casey went fer 'em. I knowed she meant 'em fer me; ye kin tell by a person's eye an' the nod o' ther head. But Casey went fer 'em, an' I give him a punch jes' back o' the ear—clear science, an' the boys made a row. While the cop was a-mendin' of their bangs I shinned it off good, I tell ye! I've run every step from Gran' Cent'al, an now I must shin off fer my papers. An' you kids kin have a picnic wid de flowers."

Patsey stopped for a breath, redder than ever in the face.

"O Patsey, you're so good!" cried the little wraith. Dil smiled through her tears, and squeezed his hand.

"Hi! good!" with a snort of merry disdain. "I jes' wisht I had the boodle to git a kerrige an' take ye both out'n the country where things grow reel in the ground, an' ye can snivy on 'em with no cop nosin' round. If Bess could walk we'd take a tower. But, tra la," and his bare feet went pattering down the stairs.

The two children looked at each other and the roses in wordless amaze. Bess ventured to touch one with her thin little fingers. Then the wail of a baby broke into their speechless delight.

There were five babies sprawling on the floor and the lounge, too near of an age to suggest their belonging to one household. Since Dil had to be kept at home with a poor sickly child who wouldn't die, Mrs. Quinn had found a way of making her profitable besides keeping the house tidy and looking after the meals. But it was not down in the lists as a day nursery.

Dilsey Quinn was fourteen. You would not have supposed her that; but hard work, bad air, and perhaps the lack of the natural joys of childhood, had played havoc with her growth and the graces of youth. She had rarely known what it was to run and shout and play as even the street arabs did. There had always been a big baby for her to tend; for the Quinns came into the world lusty and strong. Next to Dil had been a boy, now safely landed in the reform-school after a series of adventures such as are glorified in the literature of the slums. Then Bess, and two more boys, who bade fair to emulate their brother.

Mrs. Quinn was a fine, large Scotch-Irish woman; Mr. Quinn a pure son of Erin, much given to his cups, and able to pick a quarrel out of the eye of a needle. One night, four years agone, he had indulged in a glorious "shindy," smashed things in general, and little Bess in particular, beat his wife nearly to a jelly, then rushed to the nearest gin-mill, and half murdered the proprietor. He was now doing the State service behind prison-bars.

Mrs. Quinn was an excellent laundress, and managed better without him. But she, too, had a weakness for a "sup o' gin," which she always took after her day's work and before she went to bed. But woe betide the household when she began too early in the day.

The baby that set up such a howl was a fat, yellowish-white, small-eyed creature, looking like a great, soggy, overboiled potato.

"There, Jamsie, there," began the little mother soothingly; "would he like a turn in the baby-jumper? He's tired sitting on the floor, ain't he, Jamsie?"

The cooing voice and the tender clasp comforted the poor baby. She placed him in the jumper, and gave him an iron spoon, with which he made desperate lunges at the baby nearest him. But Dil fenced him off with a chair. She gave another one a crust to munch on. The two on the lounge were asleep; the other was playing with the spokes of Bess's wheel.

Dil always had a "way" with babies. It might have been better for her if she had proved less beguiling. Sometimes the number swelled to ten, but it was oftener five or six. If it fell below five there were hard lines for poor Dil, unless she had a reserve fund. She early learned the beneficent use of strategy in the way of "knock-downs."

"O Dil!" and Bess gave a long, rapturous sigh, "did you ever see so many? And they're real roses, but fine and tender and strange, somehow. The buds are like babies,—no, they're prittier than babies," glancing disdainfully at those around her; "but rose babies would be prittier and sweeter, wouldn't they?" with a wan little smile. "O my darlings, I must kiss you! Thank you a thousand, thousand times. Did the pritty lady guess you were coming to me?" She buried her face down deep in their sweetness, and every faint, feeble pulse thrilled with wordless delight.

"It was awful good of Patsey, wasn't it?" she continued, when she looked up again.

"Patsey's always good," answered Dil sententiously. She was wondering what they would do if he should get "nabbed" by any untoward accident; for every little while some boy did get "nabbed."

Patsey Muldoon smoked cigar stumps, fought like a tiger, and swore as only a street-gamin can. But he was not a thief. And to these two girls he was as loyal a knight, and brave, as any around King Arthur's Table.

"Let me untie thim. They must be hurted with the string round so tight."

Dil cut the cord, and began to unwind it. A great shower fell over Bess, who laughed softly, and uttered exclamations in every key of delight. If Virginia Deering could have witnessed the rapture of these poor things over her despised wild roses!

"O Dil, we never had so many flowers all to once!" she cried in tremulous joy. "There was the daisies from the Mission; but though they're pritty, you can't make 'em smell sweet. Do you s'pose it was over in that country you heard tell of where the beautiful lady found them? O Dil, if you could go to the Mission School again! I'd like to know some more,—oh, what will we do with them?"

Dil looked round in dismay.

"I daren't use the pitcher, and there ain't nothin' big enough. They're wilty, and they just want to be laid out straight in water. But if they're in anything, and mammy wants it, she'll just chuck thim away. Oh, dear!" and Dil glanced round in perplexity.

"Mammy promised to buy me another bowl, but she never does," was Bess's plaint.

Some one had given them a white earthen wash-bowl long before. The boys had broken it in a "tussle." They were thrashed, but Bess had not had her loss made good.

"O Bess! would you mind if I ran down to Misses Finnigan's? She might have something—cheap."

"No; run quick," was the eager response.

Dil gave a glance at the babies and was off. Around the corner in a basement was a small store of odds and ends. Mrs. Finnigan was a short, shrewd-looking woman with very red hair, a much turned-up nose, and one squint eye.

Dil studied the shelves as they were passing the time of day.

"What will wan of thim little wash-bowls cost?" she asked hesitatingly. "Bess had wan a lady sent to her, but Owny broke it. I've been looking to get her another, but it's so hard to save up a bit o' money."

"Ah, yis; so it is." Mrs. Finnigan gave the shelf a severe scrutiny. "Thim, is it now? Well, there's wan ye kin hev' fer sivin cints, dirt chape at that. It's got a bit of scale knocked off, and the dust has settled in, but it'll hould wather ivery blissid time," and she laughed with a funny twinkle in her squint eye. "Or will ye be wantin' somethin' foiner?"

"Oh, no, and I've only five cents. If you will trust me a bit"—eagerly.

"Sure I'd trust ye to Christmas an' the day afther, Dilsey Quinn. If iverybody was as honest, I'd be puttin' money in the bank where I'm bewailin' me bad debts now! Take it along wid ye."

"O Misses Finnigan, if mother should be awful about it, might I just say ye gev it to me? Mother do be moighty queer sometimes, and other whiles she don't notice."

"That I will, an' the blissid Virgin'll count it no sin. It's a long head ye've got, Dil, an' its wisdom that gets through the world widout havin' it broken. It'll be all right"—with another wink. "An' here's a bit of bananny for the poor colleen."

Dil ran off home with the bowl wrapped up in her apron to prevent incautious gossip. One of the babies was crying, but she hushed it with the end of the banana. It was rather "off," and the middle had to be amputated, but the baby enjoyed the unwonted luxury.

Then she washed her bowl and filled it with clean water.

"They'll freshen up, and the buds be comin' out every day. I'll set thim on the window-sill, and all night they'll be sweet to you between whiles, when you can't sleep. O Bess dear, do you mind the old lady who came in with her trax, I think she called thim, and sung in her trembly voice 'bout everlastin' spring an' never with'rin' flowers? I've always wisht I could remember more of it. Never with'rin' flowers! Think how lovely 'twould be!"

"An'—heaven! That's what it is, Dil. I wisht some one else could know. O Dil, think of flowers always stayin' fresh an' sweet!"

Dil snipped off the faded leaves, and gave them a fresh water bath. One branch had seven buds and five roses. The delight that stirred these starved souls was quite indescribable. Never had they possessed such a wealth of pleasure.

Now and then Dil had to leave off and comfort the fractious babies. They were getting tired, and wanted their own mothers. But for the poor little girl playing at motherhood there was no one to come in and infold her in restful arms, and comfort her when the long, warm day ended.

At last she had the bowl filled with flowers, a great mound of delicious pink and tenderest green. Bess and Dilsey knew little about artistic methods; but the sight was a joy that the finest knowledge could not have described—that full, wordless satisfaction.

A passionate pulsation throbbed in Bess's throat as if it would strangle her.

"Now," said Dil, "I'm going to set thim in your room. I'll push you in there, and you can make believe you are in a truly garden. For whin the folks come in, they'll be beggin' thim, an' they'll give thim to the babies to tear up. I couldn't abear to have thim hurted. An' babies don't care!"

"They can go out every day and see things." Bess clasped her arms about Dil's neck, and kissed her fervently.

The room was very, very small. Dil's cot stood along the wall; and there were two or three grocery boxes piled up to make a sort of closet, with a faded curtain across it. There was just room to push in the carriage by the window. It was Bess's sofa by day and bed by night. The bowl was placed on the window-sill. Now and then a breath of air found its way in.

Mrs. Finn and Mrs. Brady came in for their babies. Dil stirred the fire and put on the kettle, then washed the potatoes and set them to cook. Now and then she ran in to smile at Bess.

"It's just like heaven!" cried the little wraith.

Alas, if this was a foretaste of heaven! This close, fetid air, and the wet clothes, for they were put up at all hours. Pure air was one of the luxuries Barker's Court could not indulge in, though we talk of it being God's gift to rich and poor alike.

When the two rough, begrimed boys rushed in there was only Jamsie left; and he was in an uneasy sleep, with his thumb in his mouth, so Dil held up her hand to entreat silence. The boys lived so generally in the street, and did so much shrewd foraging, that they looked well and hearty, if they had the air of prospective toughs.

"I've put the last bit of bread in the milk for Bess's supper, and you must wait until mother comes," said Dil, with her small air of authority.

The boys grumbled. Little Dan was quick to follow Owen's lead, who said roughly,—

"O yes, de kid must have everything! An' she'll never be good fer nothin' wid dem legs. No use tryin' to fatten her up wid de luxuries o' life!" and the boy's swagger would have done credit to his father.

"She's no good," put in Dan; "'n' I'm norful hungry."

The tears came to Dil's eyes, though she was quite used to hearing such

9

remarks on the little sister she loved better than her own life. Everybody seemed to consider her such a useless burthen.

"Ain't them praties done? I could jes' eat 'em raw," whined Dan.

"Shet yer mug, er I'll gev ye a swipe," said Owen. "Ye don't look's if ye wos goin' to faint this minnit."

"You jes' mind yer own biz, Owen Quinn;" and the little fellow swelled up with an air.

Owen made a dive, but Dan was like an eel. They were on the verge of a scrimmage when their mother entered. A tall, brawny woman, with an abundance of black hair, blue eyes, and a color that, in her girlhood, had made her the belle of her native hamlet, less than twenty years ago. A hard, weather-beaten look had settled in the lines of her face, her cheeks had an unwholesome redness, her skin had the sodden aspect that hot steam brings about, and her eyes were a little bleared by her frequent potations. Her voice was loud, and carried a covert threat in it. She cuffed the boys, produced a loaf of bread, and some roast beef bones Mrs. Collins had given her.

"It just needs a stir in the kettle, Dil, for it's gone a bit sour; but it'll freshen up with salt an' some onion. How many babies?"

"Five," answered Dil.

Just then Mrs. Gillen came flying up the stairs. She was not much beyond twenty, and still comely with youth and health and hope.

"O me darlint!" snatching up her baby with rapture, "did he want his own mammy, sure?" laughing gleefully between the kisses. "Has he fretted any, Dil?"

"He's been very good." Dil was too wise to tell bad tales.

"He always is, the darlint! An' I'm late. I was ironin' away for dear life, whin Mrs. Welford comes down wid a lasht summer's gown, an' sez she, 'Mrs. Gillen, you stop an' iron it, an' I'll give ye a quarther, for ye've had a big day's work,' sez she. So what cud I do, faix, when she shpoke so cliver loike, an' the money ready to hand?"

"They're not often so free wid their tin, though heaven knows they're free enough wid their work," commented Mrs. Quinn, with a touch of contempt.

"Mrs. Welford is a rale lady, ivery inch of her. Jamsie grumbles that I go to her, but a bit o' tin comes in moighty handy. An' many's the cast-offs I do be gettin', an' it all helps. Here's five cints, and here's a nickel for yourself, Dil. Whatever in the world should we be doin' widout ye?"

"Thank you, ma'am," and Dil courtesied.

Mrs. Gillen bundled up her baby in her apron and wished them good-night, skipping home with a light heart to get her husband's supper, and hear him scold a little because she worked so late.

Mrs. Quinn held out her hand to her daughter.

"Gev me that nickel," she said.

The ready obedience was inspired more by the fear of a blow than love.

The potatoes were done, and they sat down to supper. Certainly the boys *were* hungry.

"I'm goin' to step down to Mrs. MacBride's an' sit on the stoop for a bit of fresh air," she announced. "I've worked that hard to-day there's no life left in me. Don't ye dare to stir out, ye spalpeens, or I'll break ivery blessed bone in your body," and Mrs. Gillen shook her fist by way of a parting injunction.

II—SATURDAY AFTERNOON

The boys waited until they were sure their mother was having her evening treat. Mrs. MacBride's was a very fascinating place, a sort of woman's club-house, with a sprinkling of men to make things merry. Decent, too, as drinking-places go. No dancing girls, but now and then a rather broad joke, and a song that would not appeal to a highly cultivated taste. There was plenty of gossip, but the hours were not long.

Dil washed up the dishes, dumped the stove-grate, and took the ashes out to the box. Then she swept up the room and set the table, and her day's work was done.

Patsey Muldoon came in with his heartsome laugh.

"O Patsey, they're the loveliest things, all coming up so fresh an' elegant, as if they grew in the water. Bess is wild about thim;" and Dil's tone was brimful of joy.

They went in and sat on the cot.

"They do seem alive," declared Bess, with her thin, quivering note of satisfaction. "I do be talkin' to thim all the time, as if they were folks."

Patsey laughed down into the large, eager, faded eyes.

"Sure, it's fine as a queen in her garden ye are! We'll say thanky to my lady for not kapin' them herself. An' I had a streak of luck this avenin', an' I bought the weeny thing two of the purtiest apples I could find. I was goin' to git a norange, but the cheek of 'em, wantin' five cents for wan!"

"I like the apples best, Patsey," replied the plaintive little voice. "You're so good!"

"I had one mesilf, an' it's first-rate. Casey's goin' ter lick me—don't yer wish him luck?"

Patsey laughed again. He seemed much amused over the fact.

"No, I don't," said Dil stoutly. "Was it 'bout the flowers?" and Dil began to peel the soft harvest apple, looking up with eager interest.

"The cop gev him a clip, an' he was mad all through." Patsey nodded humorously.

"What would he have done with the roses?" Dil asked, with pity in her voice.

"Taken 'em to his best gal!" This seemed an immense joke to the boy.

"An' I'm your best girl, Patsey," said Bess, laying her little hand on his, so brown.

"That you jest are, an' don't yer forgit it," he replied heartily.

Dil fed her with slices of the apple. It was so refreshing to her parched mouth and throat. Patsey had so many amusing incidents to relate; but he always slipped away early, before the boys came home. He wanted no one telling tales.

Then Dil gave Bess her evening bath, and rubbed the shrunken legs that would never even hold up the wasted body. Ah, how softly Dil took them in her hands, how tender and loving were her ministrations. All her soul went out in this one passionate affection.

"Your poor flannils is all in rags," she said pityingly. "Whatever we are to do unless some one gives mammy a lot of old stuff. O Bess! And there are such lovely ones in the stores, soft as a pussy cat."

"Mine are cool for summer." Bess gave a pitiful little laugh. Buying clothes for her was a sheer waste, in her mother's estimation.

Then Dil held the thin hands and fanned her while she crooned, in a sort of monotone, bits of beautiful sentences she had gathered in her infrequent inspection of windows where Christmas or Easter cards were displayed. She could not carry the simplest tune, to her passionate regret, but she might have improvised chanting sentences and measures that would have delighted a composer. She had transformed Bess's pillowed couch into a bed, and these hot nights she fanned her until she drowsed away herself. She used to get so tired, poor hard-worked Dilsey.

But the pathetic minor key of her untrained and as yet unfound voice Bess thought the sweetest music in the world. She was not fond of the gay, blatant street songs; her nerves were too sensitive, her ear too finely attuned to unconscious harmonies.

The tired voice faltered, the weary head drooped, the soft voice ceased.

Bess roused her.

"Dil, dear, you must go to bed. I am all nice and cooled off now, and you are so tired. Kiss me once more."

Not once but many times. Then she dropped on her own little bed and was asleep in a moment. Did God, with all his millions to care for, care also for these heathens in a great enlightened city?

It was Bess who heard the boys scuffling in and just saving themselves when their mother's heavy tread sounded in the room. It was the poor child, racked

13

by pain, whose nerves were rasped by the brawls and the crying babies, the oaths and foul language, and sometimes a fight that seemed in her very window.

Yet she lay there with her bowl of roses beside her, now and then touching them caressingly with her slight fingers, and inhaling the delicate fragrance. She was in a little realm of her own, unknowingly the bit of the kingdom of heaven within one.

But Bessy Quinn did not even know that she had a soul. There was a great hungry longing for some clean and quiet comfort, a mother she was not always afraid of, and Dil, who was never to tend babies any more. And if there could be flowers, and the "everlasting spring," and one could live out in the green fields.

They talked it over sometimes—this wonderful place they would like to find.

Morning always came too soon for Dilsey Quinn. Her mother wanted a cup of coffee, and ordered what Dil was to cook for the boys. It was a relief to see her go; but the babies began to come in at seven, and sometimes they were cross and cried after their mothers.

But on Saturday there was a great change. Mrs. Quinn washed at home; Dilsey scrubbed the floors, ironed, was maid of all work, for there was not often any babies; Mrs. Quinn did not enjoy having them around.

This afternoon she was going to "Cunny Island" with a party of choice spirits. She felt she needed an outing once a week, and five days' steady washing and ironing was surely enough. Dil helped her mother off with alacrity. This time she was unusually good-natured, and gave the children a penny all round.

Then Dil arrayed herself and Bess in their best. Dil was quite well off this summer; her mother often brought home clothes she could wear. But poor Bess had not been so fortunate. The little white cap was daintily done up, though Dil knew it would never stand another ironing. So with the dress, and the faded blue ribbon tied about her baby waist. They were scrupulously clean; one would have wondered how anything so neat could have come out of Barker's Court.

It was a feat of ingenuity for Dil's short arms to get the carriage down the narrow, winding stairs. Sometimes the boys would help, or Patsey would be there. Then she took the pillows and the faded rug, and when they were settled she carried down Bess. That was not a heavy burthen. She arranged her in a wonderful manner, pulling out the soft golden curls that were like spun silk. Bess would have been lovely in health and prosperity. Her blue eyes had black pupils and dark outside rims. Between was a light, translucent blue, changing like a sea wave blown about. The brows and lashes were dark. But the face had a wan, worn look, and the pleading baby mouth had lost its color, the features were sharpened.

One and another gave them good-day with a pleasant smile.

"It would be the Lord's mercy if the poor thing could drop off quiet like," they said to each other. It was a mystery to them how she managed to live.

They went out of the slums into heaven almost; over to Madison Square. Dil liked the broad out-look, the beautiful houses, the stores, the perspective of diverging streets, the throngs of people, the fountain, the flowers. There was an intangible influence for which her knowledge was too limited; but her inmost being felt, if it could not understand. Occasionally, like poor Joe, she was ordered to move on, but one policeman never molested her. Something in the pathetic baby face recalled one he had held in his arms, and who had gone out of them to her little grave.

Dil found a shady place and a vacant seat. She drew the wagon up close, resting her feet on the wheel. The last of the wild roses had been taken along for an airing. Poor, shrunken little buds, lacking strength to come out fully, akin to the fingers that held them so tenderly. Bess laughed at Dil's shrewd, amusing comments, and they were very happy.

Two or three long, delicious hours in this fresh, inspiriting air, with the blue sky over their heads, the patches of velvety grass, the waving trees, the elusive tints caught by the spray of the fountain, and the flowers, made a paradise for them. They drank in eagerly the divine draught that was to last them a week, perhaps longer.

A young fellow came sauntering along,—a tall, supple, jaunty-looking man, with a refined and kindly, rather than a handsome face. His hair was cropped close, there was a line of sunny brown moustache on his short upper lip, and his chin was broad and cleft. It gave him a mirthful expression, as if he might smile easily; but there was a shadow of firmness in the blue-gray eye, and now the lips were set resolutely.

He stopped and studied them. They were like a picture in their unconventional grace. He was quite in the habit of picking up odd, rustic ideas.

"Hillo!" coming nearer with a bright smile. "Where did you youngsters find wild roses? They seem not to have thriven on city air."

"*Are* they *wild* roses?" asked Dil. "What makes thim so?"

He laughed, a soft, alluring sound. Something in the quaint voice attracted him. It was too old, too intense, for a child.

"I don't know, except that they *are* wild around country places, and do not take kindly to civilization. Where I have been staying, there are hundreds of them. You can't tell much about beauty by those withered-up buds."

"O mister, we had thim when they were lovely. On Chuesday it was—Patsey Muldoon brought thim to us. And they just seemed to make Bess all alive again with joy."

The pretty suggestion of brogue, the frankness, so far removed from any aspect of boldness, interested him curiously.

"And had Patsey Muldoon been in the country?" he asked with interest.

"Oh, no. He was up to Gran' Cent'l, an' a lady who come on the train had thim. Patsey said she was beautiful and elegant, an' she gev thim to him. An' Jim Casey tried to get 'em, an' they had a scrimmage; but Patsey ain't no chump! An' he brought thim down to Bess," nodding to the pale little wraith. "Patsey's so good to us! An', oh, they was so lovely an' sweet, with leaves like beautiful pink satin, and eyes that looked at you like humans,—prittier than most humans. An' it was like a garden to us—a great bowlful. Wasn't it, Bess?"

The child smiled, and raised her eyes in exaltation. Preternaturally bright they were, with the breathless look that betrays the ebbing shore of life, yet full of eager desire to remain. For there would have been no martyrdom equal to being separated from Dil.

"O mister!" she cried beseechingly, "couldn't you tell us about them—how they live in their own homes? An' how they get that soft, satiny color? Mammy brought us home a piece of ribbon once,—some one gev it to her,— an' Dil made a bow for my cap. Last summer, wasn't it, Dil? An' the roses were just like that when we freshened them up. They was so lovely!"

He seated himself beside Dil. A curious impression came over him, and he was touched to the heart by the fondness and tender care of the roses. Was there some strange link—

"Was it Tuesday afternoon, did you say?" hesitating, with a sudden rush at his heart. "And a tall, slim girl with light hair?"

Dil shook her head with vague uncertainty. "Patsey said she was a stunner! An' she went in a kerrige. She wasn't no car folks."

He laughed softly at this idea of superiority. "Of course *you* didn't see her," he commented reflectively, with a pleasant nod. How absurd to catch at such a straw. No, he couldn't fancy *her* with a great bunch of wild roses in her slim hand, when she had so haughtily taken off his ring and dropped it at his feet.

"Oh, you wanted to know about wild roses when they were at home," coming out of his dream. What a dainty conceit it was! And he could see the pretty rose nook now; yes, it was a summer parlor. "Well, they grow about country ways. I've found them in the woods, by the streams, by the roadsides, sometimes in great clumps. And where I have been staying,—in the village of Chester,—a long distance from here, they grew in abundance. At the edge of a wood there was a rose thicket. The great, tall ones that meet over your head, and the low-growing bushy ones. Why, you could gather them by the hundreds! Have you ever been to the country?" he asked suddenly.

"We've been to Cent'l Park," answered Dil proudly.

"Well, that's the country in its Sunday clothes, dressed up for a company reception. The real country lives in every-day clothes, and gets weedy and dusty, with roads full of ruts. But you can walk on the grass; it grows all along the roadsides. Then there are flowers,—or weeds in bloom; it amounts to the same thing,—and no one scolds if you pick them. You can lie out under the trees, and the birds come and sing to you, and the squirrels run about. The air is sweet as if it rained cologne every night. Under-brush and wild blackberries reach out and shake hands with you; butterflies go floating in the sunshine; crickets sit on the stones and chirp; bees go droning by, laden with honey; and a great robin will stop and wink at you."

The children's faces were not only a study, but a revelation. John Travis thought he had never seen anything so wonderful. If a man could put such life in every feature, such exquisite bewilderment!

"What *is* a robin?" asked Bess, her face all alight with eagerness.

"A great saucy bird with black eyes and a red breast. And there is a bobolink, who flies around announcing his own name, and a tiny bird that says, 'Phebe, Phebe;' for in the country the birds can talk."

Both children sighed; their hearts were full to overflowing. What heavenly content!

"This particular spot," and John Travis's eyes seemed to look way off and soften mysteriously, "is at the edge of a wood. The road runs so," marking it out on his trousers with his finger, "way up over a sloping hill, and this one goes down to a little stream. In this angle—"

Neither of them had the slightest idea of an angle, but it did not disturb their delight.

"In this angle there are some alders and stuff, and a curious little entrance to the rose thicket. Every kind seems in a riotous tangle. The low ones that begin to bloom in June, palest pink, rose-pink, and their dainty slim buds the most

17

delicious color imaginable. There's a small cleared space; that's the parlor, with a velvety green carpet. The bushes meet overhead, and shower their soft leaves down over you. Every day hundreds of them bloom. It looks like a fairy cave. And lying down on the grass you can look up to one patch of blue sky. And I think the roses must have souls that go up to heaven—they are so sweet."

He paused in his random talk, with his eyes fixed on Dil. The rapt expression of her face transfigured her. Any one could imagine Bess being beautiful under certain healthful conditions, but Dil gave no promise to the casual glance. John Travis discerned at that moment the gift and charm higher than mere beauty, born of the soul, and visible only when the soul is deeply moved.

Her hat was pushed a little back. There was a fringe of red-brown hair with a peculiar glint, softened by the summer heat into rings. A low, broad forehead, a straight line of bronze brown, shading off in a delicate curve and fineness at the temple. But her eyes were like the gems in brown quartz, that have a prisoned gleam of sunshine in them, visible only in certain lights. Ordinarily they were rather dull; at times full of obstinate repression. Now they were illuminated with the sunrise glow. A small Irish nose, that had an amusing fashion of wrinkling up, and over which went a tiny procession of freckles. A wide mouth, redeemed by a beautifully curved upper lip, and a rather square chin that destroyed the oval.

"Hillo!" as if coming out of a dream. "See here, I'd like to sketch you—would you mind?"

He had dreamed over a picture he was to paint of that enchanted spot, a picture of happy youth and love and hope, "In Wild-Rose Time." But the dream was dead, the inspiration ended. He could never paint *that* picture, and yet so much of his best efforts had gone to the making of it! What if he arose from the ruin, and put this child in it, with her marvellous eyes, her ignorant, innocent trust, her apron full of wild roses, emerging from the shadowy hollow, and one branch caught in her hair, half crowning her.

For why should a man wreck his life on the shallows and quicksands of a woman's love? Two days ago he had said he could not paint again in years, if ever, that all his genius had been the soft glamour of a woman's smile. And here was a fresh inspiration.

Dil stared, yet the happy light did not go out of her face as she tried to grasp the mystery.

"Yes; would you mind my sketching you for a picture?"

There were not many people around. Saturday afternoons they went off on excursions. A few drowsy old fellows of the better class, two women resting and reading, waiting for some one perhaps, others sauntering.

"Oh, if you'd make a picture of Bess! She's so much prittier, an' her hair's like gold. Oh, do!" and Dil's breath came with an entreating gasp, while her face was beseeching love.

"Yes; I'll make a picture of Bess too, if you can stay long enough," he answered good humoredly.

"We can stay till dark, 'f we like. Summer nights ain't never lonesome. An' Sat'day's full of folks."

Travis laughed. "All right. Push your hat up higher—so. No, let your hair stay tumbled."

"It isn't pritty hair. They used to call me red-top, an' names. 'Tain't so red as it was."

She ran her fingers through it, and gave her head a shake.

"Capital." He had just drawn out his sketch-book, when the policeman came down with a solemn tread and authoritative countenance. But Travis nodded, and gave him an assuring smile that all was right.

"Let me see; I think I'll tell you about an old apple orchard I know. You never saw one in bloom?"

"Oh, do apples have flowers?" cried Bess. "There's never any such in the stores. What a wonderful thing country must be!"

"The blossom comes first, then the fruit." Then he began with the fascinating preface: "When I was a little boy I had been ill a long while with scarlet fever. It was the middle of May when I was taken to the country."

What a wonderful romance he made of bloom and bird music, of chickens and cows, of lambs, of the little colt that ran in the orchard, so very shy at first, and then growing so tame that the little lad took him for a playfellow. Very simple indeed, but he held his small audience entranced. The delight in Bess's face seemed to bring fine and tender expressions to that of Dil. Her nose wrinkled piquantly, her lips fell into beguiling curves. Travis found himself speculating upon the capacity of the face under the influence of cultivation, education, and happiness. He really hated to leave off, there were so many inspiring possibilities.

Now and then some one gave them a sidelong glance of wonder; but Travis went on in a steady, business-like manner; and the guardian of the square shielded them from undue curiosity.

"Bess isn't well," he said presently. "She looks like a little ghost."

"She was hurted a long while ago and she can't walk. Her little legs is just like a baby's, an' they never grow any more. But she won't grow either, and I don't so much mind so long as I can carry her."

"Will she never walk again?" he asked in surprise. "How old is she?"

"She's ten; but she's littler than the boys now, so she's the baby—the sweetest baby of thim all."

Ah, what a wealth of love spoke in the tone, in the simple words.

"I think you may take off Bess's cap," he said, with an unconsciously tender manner. Poor little girl! And yet it could not be for very long. He noted the lines made by suffering, and his heart went out in sympathy.

"Now, if there is anything you would like to ask me—anything that puzzles you"—and he reflected that most things might seem mysteries to their untrained brains.

They glanced at each other and drew long breaths, as if this was the golden opportunity they had long waited for. Then an irresistibly shy, sweet, beseeching expression crossed Bess's face, as her eyes wandered from him to her sister.

"O Dil—you might ast him 'bout—you know"—hesitating with pitiful eagerness in her large eyes—"'bout goin' to heaven, an' how far it is."

"Do you know where heaven is, mister?"

The question was asked with the good faith of utter ignorance; but there was an intense and puzzled anxiety in every line of the child's countenance.

"Heaven!" He was struck with a strange mental helplessness. "Heaven!" he repeated.

"Don't anybody know for true?" A despair quenched the sunshine in the brown eyes and made outer darkness.

"An' how they get there?" continued Bess breathlessly. "That's what we wanter know, 'cause Dil wants to go an' take me. Is it very, very far?"

Travis glanced at Dil. Never in his life had he been more at loss. There was a line between her brows, and the wrinkled nose added to the weight of thoughtfulness. Never had he seen a few wrinkles express so much.

She felt as if he was questioning her.

"I went to the Mission School, you see," she began to explain. "The teacher read about a woman who took her children an' a girl who lived with her, an' started for heaven. Then Owny took my shoes, 'cause 'twas wet an' slushy 'n' I couldn't go, an' so I didn't hear if they got there. 'N' when I went again, that teacher had gone away. I didn't like the new wan. When I ast her she said it was a gory somethin', an' you didn't go that way to heaven now."

"An allegory, yes."

"Then, what's that?"

"A story of something that *may* happen, like every-day events." Ah, how could he meet the comprehension of these innocent children?

"Well, did she get there?" with eager haste.

The sparrows went on with their cheerful, rather aggressive chirp. The fountain played, people passed to and fro, and wagons rumbled; but it seemed to John Travis as if there were only themselves in the wide world—and God. He did not understand God, but he knew then there was some supreme power above man.

"Yes," with reverent gentleness, "yes, she found heaven."

"Then, what's to hinder us, Dil? 'Twouldn't be any use to ast mother—she'd rather go to Cunny Island or Mis' MacBride's. If you only would tell us the way—"

"Yes; if you *could* tell us the way," said Dil wistfully, raising her entreating eyes.

Could he direct any one on the road to heaven? And then he admitted to himself that he had cast away the faint clew of years agone, and would not know what step to take first.

"You see," explained Dil hurriedly, "I thought when we'd found just how to go, I'd take Bess some Sunday mornin', an' we'd go up by Cent'l Park and over by the river, 'cause they useter sing 'One more river to cross.' Then we'd get on a ferry-boat. Mother wouldn't care much. She don't care for Bess since she's hurted, and won't never be no good. But I could take care of her; an' when we struck the right way, 'twould be just goin' straight along. I could scrub an' 'tend babies an' sweep an' earn some money. People was good to the woman in the story, an' mebbe they'd be good to us when we were on the road an' no mistake. If we could just get started."

Oh, the eager, appealing desire in her face, the faith and fervor in her voice! A poor little pilgrim, not even knowing what the City of Destruction meant, longing with all her soul to set out for that better country, and take her poor little crippled sister. It moved him beyond anything he had ever known, and blurred the sunshine with a tremulous mistiness.

Dil was watching the varying expressions.

"O mister, ain't there any heaven? Will we have to go on living in Barker's Court forever 'n' ever?"

The despair in Dil's voice was heartrending. John Travis thought he had passed one hour of crucial anguish; but it was as nothing to this, inasmuch as the pang of the soul must exceed the purely physical pain. He drew a long, quivering breath.

"Oh, there ain't any!"

He was on the witness stand. To destroy their hope would be a crueler murder than that of the innocents. No, he dared not deny God.

III—THE WAY TO HEAVEN

John Travis was like a good many young men in the tide of respectable church-going. His grandmother was an old-fashioned Christian, rather antiquated now; but he still enjoyed the old cottage and the orchard of long ago. His mother was a modern church member. They never confessed their experiences one to another in the fervent spiritual manner, but had clubs and guilds and societies to train the working-people. She was interested in charitable institutions, in homes, and the like; that is, she subscribed liberally and supervised them. Personally she was rather disgusted with the inmates and their woes, whose lives and duties were mapped out by rule, whether they fitted or not.

Then, he had two sisters who were nice, wholesome, attractive girls, who danced all winter in silks and laces, kept Lent rigorously with early services, sewing-classes, and historical lectures, and took their turns in visiting the slums. All summer there was pleasuring. The young women in their "set" were much alike, and he wondered who of them all could show these little waifs the way to heaven.

For himself, he had gone through college honorably. He was a moral young man, because a certain fine, clean instinct and artistic sense forbade any excesses. To be sure, he had read Strauss and Renan after his Darwin and Spencer, he had even dipped into the bitter fountains of Schopenhauer. He had a jaunty idea that the myths and miracles of the Bible were the fables and legends of the nations in the earlier stages of their development, quite outgrown in these later days of exact philosophical reasoning.

But as he sat there, with these children's eyes fixed upon him with an intent life-and-death expression, uttering a strong, inward soul cry that reached his ears and would not be shut out, a certain assurance came to him. These tender little souls were waiting for the word that was to lead them in the way of life everlasting. "Whoso offendeth one of these little ones"—it was there in letters of fire.

What but heaven could compensate them for their dreary lives here! What but the love of God infold them when father and mother had failed. For surely they had not demanded any part in the struggle of life. Ah, if the dead rose not again—what refinement of cruelty to send human beings into the world to suffer like brutes, having a higher consciousness to intensify it ten-fold, and then be thrust into the terrible darkness of nothingness. Even *he* was not willing to come to a blank, purposeless end.

He had been sketching rapidly, but he saw the little faces changing with an uncomprehended dread. Dil's sunshine was going out in sullen despair. Yes, he *must* bear witness—for to-day, for all time, for all human souls. In that moment he believed. A rejoicing, reverent consciousness was awakened within him; and the new man had been born, the man who desired to learn the way to heaven, even as these little children.

"Yes, there *is* a heaven." He could feel the tremulousness in his voice, yet the assurance touched him with inexpressible sweetness, so new and strange was it. "There is a God who cares for us all, loves us all, and who has prepared a beautiful land of rest where there is no pain nor sorrow, where no one is sick or lonely or in any want, where the Lord Jesus gathers the sorrowing into his arms, and wipes away their tears, soothes them with his own great love, which is sweeter and tenderer than the best human love."

"Oh," cried Dil, as he paused, "are you jest certain sure? There was a little old lady who came and sang once 'bout a beautiful country, everlastin' spring, an' never with'rin' flowers. I didn't get the hang of it all, but it left a sort of sweetness in the air that you could almost feel, you know. Don't you b'lieve she knew 'bout the truly heaven?"

Dil's brown eyes were illumined again.

"Yes—that was heaven." His grandmother sang that old hymn. He would go up there and learn it some day, and tell her that in the midst of the great city he had borne witness to the faith. The knowledge was so new and strange that it filled him with great humility, made him a little child like one of these.

"Oh," cried Dil, with a long, restful sigh of satisfaction, while every line of her face was transfigured, "you must know, 'cause, you see, you've had chances. You can read books and all. And now I am quite sure—Bess an' me," placing her hand lovingly over the little white one. "An' mebbe you c'n tell us just how to go. And when you come to the place, there's a bridge or something that people get over, and go up beyond the sky—jest back of the blue sky," with a certain confident, happy emphasis in the narrow, but rapt, vision.

"Couldn't we start right away?" cried Bess with eager hopefulness, her wan little face in a glow of excitement. "What's the good o' goin' back home? Me an' Dil have talked it over an' over. An' there must be crowds an' crowds goin',—people who are strong and well, an' can run. Why, I sh'd think they'd be in an awful hurry to get there. An' you said no one would be sick. My head aches so when the babies cry, an' my poor back is so tired an' sore. Oh, if I had two good legs, so Dil wouldn't have to push me an' lift me out an' in! O Dil, do let's go!"

She was trembling with excitement, and her eyes were a luminous glow.

What could John Travis say to these eager pilgrims? He did not remember that he had ever known any one in a hurry to get to heaven. How strange it was! And how could he explain this great mystery of which he knew so little, —the walk that was by faith, not sight?

"You said you had been to the Mission School," catching at that straw eagerly. "Did they not tell you—teach you"—and he paused in confusion.

"I ain't been much. Mammy don't b'lieve in thim. An' I think they don't know. One tells you one thing, an' the nex' one another. One woman said the sky was all stars through an' through, an' heaven was jest round you, an' where you lived. Well, if it's Barker's Court," and she made a strange, impressive pause, "'tain't much like the place the woman set out for."

"She left the City of Destruction. Her name was Christiana."

"Oh, yes!" kindling anew with awakened memory. "Well, that's Barker's Court. There's fightin', an' swearin', an' gettin' drunk, an' bein' 'rested. Poor Bess hears 'em in the night when she can't sleep. An' the woman went away, an' took her children. But mammy wouldn't go, an' we'll have to start by our two selves. O mister! do you know anything 'bout prayin'? The teacher told me how, an' I prayed 'bout Bess's poor legs, an' that mother'd let rum alone, an' not go off into tantrums the way pop uster. An' it didn't do a bit o' good."

She looked up so perplexed. This was not scientific or philosophical ignorance,—he could find arguments to combat that; it was not unwillingness to try, but the utter innocent ignorance, with the boundary of certain literal experiences. But how could he explain? From the depths of his heart he cried for wisdom.

"It is a long journey, and the summer is almost gone," he said, after some consideration. "The cold weather will be here presently, and you are both so little; suppose you wait until next spring? I will find you that book about Christiana, and you can learn a good many things—and be getting ready—"

He knew he was paltering with a miserable subterfuge; but, oh! what could he say? Surely, ere violets bloomed again and buttercups were golden, Bess would have solved the great mystery. Ah, to think of her as well and rejoicing in heaven! It moved all one's heart in gratitude.

Both children looked pitifully disappointed. Bess was first to recover. The tears shone in her eyes as she said,—

"Well, le's wait. My clo'es is most worn out, an' the cold pinches me up so, Dil, you know. An' it'll be nice to find how Christiana went. How'll we get the book?"

"I will bring it to you," he promised.

"An' will there be wild roses in heaven?" Bess fingered the poor faded buds as if her conscience suddenly smote her.

"All beautiful things; and they will not wither in that divine air."

She pressed them against her cheek with a touch so tender he could have blessed her for it. And there came the other vision of the soft white fingers that had torn them so ruthlessly in her anger; of the hot, passionate words! Would she forgive if he went to her, or would she tread his olive branch in the dust?

"Tell me something about yourselves;" and he roused from his dream abruptly. "Where is your father?"

"'Twas him that hurted Bess's legs, an' he got jugged for it. He beat mammy dreadful—he uster when he had the drink in him. An' now mammy's goin' the same way. That's why I'd like to take Bess somewhere—"

"Are there just you two?"

"There's Owen an' Dan. They're little chaps, but they'd get along. Boys soon get big enough to strike back. An' some one else 'ud have to look out for the babies."

"Babies! How many?" in amaze.

"I keep thim when their mothers go to work. Sometimes they're cross, and it's dreadful for poor Bess."

"And your mother allows you to do that?"

"She's got ter!" cried Bess, her smouldering indignation breaking out. "An' keep the house. An' when there's only two or three mother swears she'll send Dil to the shop to work. So we'd rather have thim, for it would be dreadful for me to be without Dil, don't you see?"

Yes, he saw, and his heart ached. He had a vague idea of some of the comfortable homes, but to be without Dil! "Did his mother and sisters ever meet with any such lives, and such tender devotion?" he wondered. It was enough to break one's heart. It almost broke his to think he could not rescue them. The picturesque aspects of poverty had appealed to him in the street-gamins and ragged old men who besieged him for "tin cints fer a night's lodgin'," that he knew would be spent for whiskey in the nearest saloon; but of the actual lives of the very poor he had but the vaguest idea.

"And your mother?" he ventured, dreading the reply.

"She goes out washin'. 'Tisn't so very bad, you see," returned Dil, with a certain something akin to pride. "Beggin's worse."

He had finished the sketches,—there were several of them,—and he began to gather up his pencils.

"Now that the work is done, we must have a picnic," he said cheerfully. "I'll find a fruit-stand somewhere. Keep right here until I return."

The children gazed at each other in a sort of speechless wonder. There were no words to express the strange joy that filled each heart. Their eyes followed him in and out, and even when he was lost to sight their faith remained perfect. Then they looked at each other, still in amazement.

"It's better'n Cunny Island," said Bess. "I've wisht we could go sometime when mother's startin' out. But if she'd been good an' tooken us, we wouldn't a' seen *him*. But I'm kinder sorry not to start right away, after all. Only there's the cold, an' I ain't got no clo'es. Mebbe he knows best. An' he's so nice."

"It's curis," Dil said after a long pause. "I wisht I could read quick an' had some learnin'. There's so many things to know. There's so many people in the world, an' some of thim have such nice things, an' can go to places—"

"Their folks don't drink rum, mebbe," returned the little one sententiously.

"I don't s'pose you can get out of it 'cept by goin' to heaven. But then, why— mebbe the others what's havin' good times don't care to go. Mebbe he won't," drearily.

He soon returned with a bag of fruit. Such pears, such peaches, and bananas! And when he took out his silver fruit-knife, pared them, and made little plates out of paper, their wonder was beyond any words.

Dil eyed hers askance. She was so used to saving the best.

"Oh, do eat it," cried Bess. "You never tasted anything like it! O mister, please tell her to. She's alwers keepin' things for me."

"There will be plenty for you to take home. I must find you some flowers too. And this evening I am going to start on a journey—to be away several weeks. I'm sorry to lose sight of you, and I want to know how to find Barker's Court. When I come back—would your mother mind your posing for me, do you think?"

"Posing?" Dil looked frightened.

"Just what you did this afternoon. Being put in a picture."

It had suddenly come into his mind that he could lighten Dil's burthen that way. He wanted to keep track of them.

"And what do you do with the pictures?"

"Sell them"—and he smiled.

"You couldn't sell me; I'm not pritty enough," she said, with the utter absence of all personal vanity, and a latent sense of amusement.

"When I come back we will talk about it. And I will bring you the book. You will learn more than I can tell you. I used to read it when I was a boy. And then we will talk about—going to heaven."

He colored a little, and his heart beat with a new and unwonted emotion.

"You're quite sure we can go nex' spring?" queried Bess. "Do many people live there?"

"The Lord Jesus Christ and all his angels," he answered reverently. "And the saints who have been redeemed, little children, and a multitude no man can number."

A perplexing frown settled between Dil's eyes.

"Seems as if I couldn't never get the thing straight 'bout—'bout Jesus Christ," and a flush wavered over her face. "When the people in the court get drunk and fight, they swear 'bout him. If he jest gives people strength to beat and bang each other, how can he help 'em to be good? Maybe there's more than one. An' why don't the one who lives in the beautiful heaven have a different name. I ast the Mission teacher once, an' she said I was a wicked girl. Mammy said there wasn't any God at all. How do *you* know?"

There was a brave, eager innocence in her eyes, and a curious urgency as well.

"'Cause," she subjoined, "if God lives in heaven and keeps it for people, if there wasn't any God, there couldn't be any heaven. Some folks in the court have the Virgin Mary, but I never see God."

There was no irreverence in her tone, but a perplexed wonder. And John Travis was helpless before it. How did the missionaries who went to the heathen ever make them understand? They had their idols of wood and stone, and had prayed to them; but this child had no God, not even an idol, though she loved Bess with every fibre of her being.

And he had almost said in his heart, "There is no God." A first great cause, an atom rushing blindly about the darkness for another atom, a protoplasm, a long series of evolutions—how complacent he had been about it all! Could he teach these children science? He had heard the talk of the slums occasionally, blood-curdling oaths, threats, wishes, curses hurled at one another. These two little girls lived in it. Could any one enlighten them, unless they were taken to a new, clean world? Yet their souls seemed scarcely soiled by the contact, their faces bore the impress of purity.

Was it thus when the Lord came in the flesh, when the wickedness of the world was very great, its hopelessness well nigh fatal? He found many ignorant souls; but they learned of him and believed, and went forth to convert the world. Was it so much more wicked now?

"Let me tell you about the true Jesus," he said in a soft, low tone, almost afraid to bear witness, he was so ignorant himself. "Long ago, when people were full of sorrow and suffering, and had forgotten how to be good to each other, God, who lived in this beautiful heaven, sent his Son down to teach them. He came and lived among them and helped them. Why, my little Dil, it's just like your caring for Bess. She can never do anything to pay you back. She cannot sweep the house, nor tend the babies, nor sew, nor earn money. But you do it because you love her, and you only want love in return. She gives it to you."

Dil stared stupidly. "I don't want her to do nothin'," she said, with a quivering lip.

"But you want her to love you."

"How could I help it?" cried Bess.

"No, you couldn't. And when the Lord found people ill and lame and blind, he cured them—"

"O mister!" interrupted Bess, with her face in a glow of wonderful light, "do you s'pose he could have cured my poor hurted little legs so's I could walk on 'em agen?"

"Yes, my child. He would have taken you in his arms and laid his hand on you, and you would have been strong and well."

"And where is he now?" she asked eagerly.

"He went back to heaven—to his Father." Ah, how could he explain to their limited understanding the sacrifice that had redeemed the world. He began to realize that faith for one's self was easier than giving a reason for one's faith. "He told people how to be kind and tender and loving, and to care for those in pain and sickness. He begged them to do it because he had loved them. That was all he wanted back. But there were ungrateful people, and those who were eager to fight and destroy each other, and they would not listen to him. But when he went away he left others, teachers, and they go on telling people —"

How could he make it simple enough for their comprehension? He was in despair.

"Then he called those together who loved him and were willing to be good and kind, and said to them, 'In my Father's house are many mansions—I go to prepare a place that you may be with me'—"

"And that's heaven," interrupted Bess, her eyes shining and her lips pink and quivering. "O Dil! that's where we are to go. I can't hardly wait till spring. An' soon's we get there, I'll ast him to cure my poor little legs poppy hurted when he threw me 'gainst the wall. Oh, are you sure, sure he will, so I can run about agen? Seems jes' too good to happen."

"Yes, I am sure. He took little children in his arms and blessed them when they crowded around him so that people would have driven them away. And he said, 'I have a heaven for all those who suffer, all those whose parents beat or maim or starve them. I will take them to my beautiful home, and they shall never suffer any more. They shall roam in lovely gardens and gather flowers, and sing and love and obey me, and be happy.'"

"O Dil, *will* you mind if I love this Lord Jesus? For he is so good I can't help it. I shall always love *you* best. I will tell him how it was—that you loved me when there wasn't any one else, and mammy wanted me to die 'cause I was so much trouble. An', Dil, don't you b'lieve he will say that was jest the kind of love he preached about, and 'cause you did it you must have a place right by me?"

The tears came to John Travis's eyes. He wondered if the Master had ever been rewarded with a more exquisite joy.

Dil squeezed her hand.

"Oh," cried Bess, "when we start to go to heaven in the spring, won't you go along? We'd like to have you so. Don't they have grown-up men in heaven? You're so nice an' clean an' different from most folks, I sh'd think you'd like to go."

"Yes, I will," in the tone of one who gives a sacred promise. When he came to think of it, very few people had asked him to go to heaven.

"Seems too good to be true," said Dil sententiously. "Good things mos'ly ain't true. An' it all seems so strange—"

"We'll talk it over while we are going to heaven," he said with grave sweetness, glancing at his watch and amazed at the lateness. "I will bring you Christiana, and when you have read that I can explain many things to you. I shall have to go now. Tell me how to find Barker's Court when I come back."

"You won't like it," Dil exclaimed sharply. "It's dirty an' horrid, full of women washing clo'es, an' drunken people, an' swearin'. Oh, let me bring Bess over here. And the picture—"

"You shall have that. But I can't tell just when I shall be able to come. Never fear but I'll find you. Here is something because you and Bess posed."

It was a five-dollar note. Dil drew back in dismay.

"O mister, I couldn't take it. I'm afeard some one'd think I stole it—so much money!"

He changed the bill into smaller ones. Then he slipped it into the bag of fruit.

"This is Bess's bank," he said, with a friendly, trusty smile. "When she wants any delicacies, you must spend the money for them. It is Bess's secret, and you must not tell any one."

He thrust the bag at the foot of the shabby carriage, and then pressed both hands.

"You're so lovely, so splendid," sighed Bess.

He picked up three withered buds—had some hands very dear to him held them?

"Good-by. I shall find Barker's Court and you, never fear." Then he plunged into the crowd, not daring to look back. What a week it had been, beginning with sorrow and loss, and—had he found the Master? Had these strange, brave little heathens, who knew not God, opened his eyes and his heart to that better way?

IV—THE DELIGHTS OF WEALTH

The children sat there in a maze of bewilderment. They knew nothing of fairy godmothers, or Santa Claus, or the dainty myths of childhood. Four years Bess had been in prison, twice four years Dilsey Quinn had been a bound slave. Not that Mrs. Quinn had been hard above all mothers. In the next house there were two little girls who sat and sewed from daylight to dark, and had no Saturday even, the age of Owen and Bess. Barker's Court was an industrious place for children, at least. If they could have played when the men were sleeping off orgies, or the women gossiping, they would have had many a respite from toil.

This wonderful thing that had befallen Bess and Dil was so beyond any event that had ever happened before, and their imaginations were so limited, they could never have dreamed such a romance. John Travis had disappeared in the throng. But there was the bag of fruit, and the sweet knowledge that nothing could take away.

The roar of vehicles had grown less. Pedestrians were thinning out, for supper-time was drawing nigh. The shadows were lengthening; the wind had a certain grateful coolness. Still they sat as in a trance. The "cop" had received a "tip" to keep a kindly watch over them, but he would have done it without any reward.

"Dil!" The soft voice broke the hush, for it was as if they two were alone in the crowd.

The little fingers closed over the firm brown ones. They looked at each other for some moments with grave, wondering eyes. Then Dil rose soberly, settled Bess anew, and pushed the wagon along. The paper bag lay in plain sight, but no one molested it.

Dil began to come back to her narrow, practical world. Heaven, as John Travis had put it, was something for Bess rather than herself. It was too great a feast to sit down to all at once. And Dil was not much used to feasting, even playing at it with bits of broken crockery and make-believes, as so many children do. They left the enchanted country behind them, and returned to more familiar sights and sounds. Still, the delicious fragrance of the pears, the flavor of the peaches, the sweetness of the candy, was so much beyond the treats over on the East Side.

"Bess," she said, stopping at a show window on the avenue, "jes' look at the caps an' things. Do you s'pose it's real money in the bag? For it's yours, an' you do need a new cap. That old one'll hardly hold together. If some one doesn't give mammy a pile of things pritty soon, you'll have to go naked."

They both laughed. "O Dil! wasn't it splendid?" and Bess turned her head around, as if she might still see their beneficent friend.

"Let me feel in my bank," she said.

Dil handed her the bag, full of fruity fragrance. She drew out a bill with a fearful little gesture.

"They're good, all of 'em," she said reassuringly. "He wouldn't give us bad money to get us into trouble. An' we never have any real money to spend."

Still Dil eyed the bill doubtfully.

"An' flannils, an' O Dil, couldn't you buy *one* new dress? I'd like to have a spandy new one for onct."

"I s'pose mother wouldn't know when onct it was washed. An' I might crumple down the bows on the cap. O Bess, you'd look so sweet! I wisht you'd had a new cap to-day. He said 'twas your money. An' I was most afear'd it was like thim things Patsey told about, when you raised the han'kercher they wasn't there!"

"But they're here." She laughed with soft exultation. "Le's go in, Dil. I never went shoppin' in my life! You could hide the things away from mammy. There'd be no use givin' it to her. She's got enough for gin an' to go to Cunny Island an' MacBride's. But jinky! wouldn't she crack our skulls if she *did* know it. O Dil, let's never, *never* tell."

"She couldn't make me tell if she killed me."

"Le's go in. Can you carry me?"

She drew the wagon up by the corner of the show-window, and, taking Bess in her arms, entered the store and seated her on a stool, standing so she could brace the weak little back. Of the few dreams that had found lodgment in Dil's prosaic brain, was this of indulging her motherly, womanly instinct, shopping for Bess. She felt dazed to have it come true. Her face flushed, her breath came irregularly, her heart beat with a delicious, half-guilty pleasure.

There was no one else in the store. A pale, tired, but kindly-looking woman came to wait on her. Dil tried on caps with laces and ribbons, and Bess looked so angelic it broke her heart to take them off. But the plain ones were less likely to betray them. Then they looked at dresses and the coveted "flannils," and one nice soft petticoat, and oh, some new stockings.

A shrewd little shopper was Dil. She counted up every purchase, and laid aside the sum, really surprised at her bargains and the amount she had left. The attendant was very sympathetic, and inquired what had befallen Bess. Dil said she had been hurted by a bad fall, that her mother was 'most always out to work, and that they hadn't any father. She was afraid her mother might be washing somewhere, and hear the story, if she was too explicit.

"Le's buy a han'kercher for Patsey," suggested Bess, her pale face in a glow.

They chose one with a pink border, thinking of the wild roses that had brought such great good luck.

"And here is a blue belt ribbon for the little girl," said the lady. "It's been in the window, and has two faded places, but you can tie them in the bow."

Dil had been struggling between economy and a belt ribbon. She raised her brown eyes so full of delight that words were hardly needed.

They packed up their goods and departed. Bess wore her cap, and held up her head like a real lady. I doubt if there were two happier children in the whole city.

Dusk was beginning to fall; but all the stores were in a glow, and now people were coming out again after supper. They seldom stayed this late, but to-night they were quite safe. And oh, how splendid it all was! the happiness of a lifetime.

Bess kept turning partly round and talking out her delight. Pain and weariness were forgotten. They laughed in sheer gladness. If John Travis could have seen them, he would have said he had never in his life made such an investment of five dollars.

"And we've only spent a little over two. Oh, what a lot of things you can buy when you have some money! An', Dil, we'll put away a good bit, so's when there ain't many babies mother won't bang you. Oh, she'd kill us both dead an' take the money if she knew, wouldn't she?"

"She would that," subjoined Dil grimly.

Poor Dil had been banged pretty severely in her short day. Last spring Mrs. Quinn had been complained of, as the "banging" had been so severe that Dil had fainted, and had to keep her bed several days.

"Oh, I wisht we wasn't ever going home," sighed Bess. "If I had two good legs we'd run away like that Mullin girl. An' now that I've got some clo'es, I'm sorry we can't go right off. Nex' spring—how many months, Dil?"

August was almost ended. Seven long, weary months at the best.

"There's Thanksgivin' an' Christmas, an'—an' St. Patrick's; that's in March, I know. An' after that it gen'ally comes warm. Oh, it seems as if I couldn't wait! But the man will come with Christiana, an' then we'll find how to go without gettin' lost or makin' a mistake. Ain't it queer? I should think everybody'd want to go."

The big eyes were full of wonder.

"Well, you see the people who have money an' things an' flowers an' journeys an' live in grand houses don't need to be in a hurry. 'Tain't of so much account to them. An' I guess people haven't got the straight of it, someway."

Poor Dil! She wasn't very straight in her own mind. If God could give people so much, why didn't he do it now? Or if they had to go to heaven for it, why wasn't it made plain, and you could be let to start whenever you desired?

Bess's confidence gave her a curiously apprehensive feeling. Suppose there wasn't any heaven? The mystery was incomprehensible.

It was late when they reached home. Oh, the sickening heat and smells! But at this hour on Saturday night the court was comparatively quiet. The revelry began later.

Dan sat on the stoop crying. He had been in a fight, and the under dog at that, and had one black eye, and his jacket torn to ribbons.

"An' mother'll wollop me for the jacket," he whimpered.

"Come an' have yer eye tied up with cold water. I did a bit of work this afternoon, an' got some goodies, an' you shall have some. Oh, it's pritty bad, Dan. Take my penny an' go buy an oyster,—that'll help get the black out."

Dan was mightily tempted to spend the penny otherwise, but the thought of the goodies restrained him. Dil took Bess and the "treasures" up-stairs, and laid her gently on the old lounge. She had everything put away when Dan returned, so she washed his face and bound up his eye.

He ceased sniffling, and cried, "O golly!" at the sight of two luscious bananas. "Dil, ye wor in luck! I didn't even see a chance to snivy on an apple. Store folks is mighty s'picious, watchin' out."

"O Dan! It's wicked to steal!"

"None o' yer gals' gaff!" said Dan with his mouth full. "Snivyin' somethin' ter eat ain't no stealin'. An' I'm hungry as an elefunt."

Dil fixed him some supper, and he devoured it with the apparent capacity of the elephant. Then, as he was very tired and used up, he tumbled on his straw pallet in his mother's room, and in five minutes was asleep.

Now the young conspirators had to consider about a hiding-place for their unaccustomed treasures.

"I'll tell you," and Bess laughed shrewdly, "we'll make a bank under the cushion of the wagon." At the risk of smothering Dan, they had shut his door. "Mother wouldn't dast to tumble me out, and no one *knows*. An' we'll call it somethin' else. We'll never say m——"

"Yes." Dil put it in the paper bag, and then she made the night bed on top of it. What a fortune it was! They glanced furtively at each other, as if questioning their right to it.

"Mammy seldom *does* look round," said Dil; "an' I'll clear the room up on Fridays, I sometimes do. An' I'll tell her I made the dress, if she spies it out. No, that would be a lie, an' tellin' lies roughs you up inside, though sometimes it's better than bein' banged. Bess, dear, I wish it was all true 'bout heaven."

"It is true, I feel it all over me."

Poor Dil sighed softly. She wasn't so sure.

Then she bathed Bess, and threw away the ragged garments. Bess was tired, but bright and happy. They stowed away their purchases, and were all settled when Owen came in. No one would have guessed the rare holiday.

Barker's Court was beginning its weekly orgy—singing, swearing, dancing, fighting, and fortunate if there was not an arrest or two. But Dil was so tired that she slept through it all, forgetting about the money, and not even haunted by dreams.

It was past midnight when Mrs. Quinn returned, to find everything still within. She tumbled across her bed, and slept the sleep of a drunken woman until Sunday noon.

Dil looked after the breakfast. Dan's eye was much improved. Out of an old bundle she found a jacket a size or two beyond him, but the children of the slums are not critical. The boys went out to roam the streets. Patsey sidled in with a knowing wink towards Mrs. Quinn's chamber door. It was nearly always safe on Sunday morning. He had a handful of flowers.

They gave him his "hankercher." But somehow they couldn't tell him of their adventure.

"But yous oughtn't 'er spend yer tin on me," he said with awkward gratefulness. "Yous don't have much look fer scrapin' it up."

"But you're alwers so good to us," returned Bess, in her sweet, plaintive tone.

"An' when yous want a nickel or two, let me know," he said with manly tenderness.

Dil made her mother a cup of strong coffee, and brushed out her long black hair, still handsome enough for a woman of fashion to envy. She had made a big Irish stew for dinner, and when the house was cleared up, she had leave to take Bess out. But they did not go to the square to-day. They rambled up and down some of the nicer streets, where the houses were closed and the people away, and speculated about the journey to heaven in the spring. Alas! There were hundreds more who did not even know there was a heaven, or for what the church bells rang, or why Sunday came.

The week was melting hot. One of the babies had a very sick day, and died that night. Several others in the court died, but the summer was always hard on babies. Mrs. Quinn had a day off, and went up to Glen Island. Children and babies were taken away for a day or a week; but Dil was too busy, and it would have been no pleasure for Bess to go without her. But some way they were overlooked.

The heat kept up well in September. People came home from the country, and Mrs. Quinn's business was brisk enough. The boys were sent to school; but Owen often played "hookey," and was getting quite unmanageable, in fact, a neighborhood terror.

It seemed strange indeed that Bess could live under such circumstances. But Dil's love and care were marvellous. She kept the child exquisitely clean; she even indulged in a bottle of refreshing cologne, and some luxuries, for which they blessed John Travis. Three times they had been over to the square. They counted up the weeks; they believed with all possible faith at first, then Dil weakened unconsciously. She used to get so tired herself in these days. Her mother was very captious, and the babies fell off. Some days Dil put in two nickels out of her precious fund. Bess insisted upon it.

Dilsey Quinn ran out of an errand now and then. She was too busy ever to loiter, and every moment away from Bess was torture. So, although they lived in a crowd, they might as well have been on a desert island, as far as companionship went.

And now they saw less of Patsey, to their sorrow. He had saved up a little money, and borrowed some from a good friend, and bought a chair, and set himself up in business. Not a mere common little "kit," mind you. But it was way down town, and he had new lodgings to be "handy."

The last of September the weather, that had been lovely, changed. There was a long, cold storm, and blustering winds that would have done credit to March. The "flannils," that had been such a luxury, were too thin, and Dil spent almost her last penny for some others. No one had ever found out.

How often they looked wistfully at each other, and asked a wordless question. But John Travis had not found them, had not come. Six weeks since that blissful Saturday!

It had been a very hard day for Dil; and heaven seemed far off, as it does to many of us in times of trouble. The morning was lowering and chilly. Dil had overslept, and her mother's morning cup of coffee was not to her taste. She had given her a box on the ear, I was about to say; but her mother's hand covered the whole side of her head, and filled it with a rush as of many waters, blinding her eyes so that all looked dark about her. Then Mrs. Kenny's little Mamie cried for her mother, and would not be pacified. Mrs. Kenny was a young and deserted wife who worked in a coat-shop, and Mamie was a Saturday boarder as well. Dil made the boys' breakfast with the baby in her arms, and managed to get Bess's bread and milk, but had hardly a moment to devote to her. Only one more baby came in.

Mrs. Quinn suddenly reappeared. Mrs. Watson had been called away by the illness of her mother, and the washing was to go over to the next week.

"An' she'll want two days' work done in one, an' no more pay. An' they don't mind about *your* lost day! How's a woman to live with a great raft of young ones to support, I'd like to know? An' it's hard times we hear about a'ready. Goodness knows what I'll do. An' you lazy trollop! you haven't your dishes washed yet! An' only two babies! Yer' not worth yer salt!"

"Mamie has cried all the time—"

"Shet yer head! Not a word of impidence out of you, or I'll crack yer skull! An' I know—yer've been foolin' over that wretched little brat in there! I'm a fool fer not sindin' her up to th' Island hospital. Fine work they'd have with her! She'd get nussed."

Dil uttered a cry of terror.

Her mother caught her by the shoulder, and banged her head sharp against the wall, until no telescope was needed for her to see stars, even in the day time. They swirled around like balls of fire, and Dil staggered to a chair, looking so ghastly that her mother was startled.

Both babies set up a howl.

"Drat the brats!" she cried, shaking her fist at them. "If there can't be more than two, you'll march off to a shop, Dilsey Quinn; an' if you don't earn your bread, you won't get it, that's all! As fer you, ye little weasened-face, broken-backed thing, cumberin' the ground—"

Bess seemed to shrink into nothing. Mrs. Quinn had taken her glass of gin too early in the day. What would have happened next—but a rap on the door averted it.

"O Mrs. Quinn!" cried Mrs. Malone, "I saw ye comin' back, an' have ye no work the day?"

"My folks went off. If I'd known last night"—Mrs. Quinn picked up one baby to hush it.

"Well, now, Ann come in a moment ago to hunt up a la'ndress. The big folks where she lives have been lift in the lurch with ivry blissid thing sprinkled down. An' can ye go an' iron fer 'em? It's a foine place. Two days in a week, an' good pay. But the la'ndress has grown that sassy they had a reg'lar shindy this mornin'. If ye'll jist go for wanst, they'll all be moighty glad, for it's a fine ironer ye are, Mrs. Quinn."

"I'll go back wid Ann." Mrs. Quinn dropped the baby, and resumed her hood and shawl.

Bess shivered, and stretched out her arms to Dil as soon as the door closed.

"Oh, what should we have done if she had stayed at home! She looked at me so dreadful. And she would have shaked the very life out of me if she had taken hold of me. O Dil, don't let her send me away!"

"If she should—if she did—I'd—I'd kill her!" and a fierce, desperate look came in the brown eyes. "O Bess dear, don't cry so, don't cry."

"O Dil," sobbed the child, "then you'd be jugged like daddy, but you wouldn't kill her—you couldn't, she's so much bigger an' stronger."

"But I'd fight awful! And I wouldn't stay. I'd run away, if I had to drown myself."

"They cut people up in hospitals"—and there was an awesome sound in the frightened voice.

"Don't, dear, don't;" and the pleading was that of agony. She held Bess close —all her life was centred in this poor, maimed body. The babies might cry, the world might cease to be, but nothing should part them.

"She'll be cross because there ain't more babies. And to-day she knows. But the bank's most all out. O Dil, s'pose something happened to—to him!"

They looked at each other in a pathetic fashion through their tears, each bearing the other's sorrow, though they knew nothing of the divine injunction. Dil had fought silent battles with herself for faith in John Travis, but Bess had never wavered until now.

"It was so beautiful—that afternoon, an' the talkin'. I've thought so often 'bout his Lord Jesus, who could make my poor little legs well, an', Dil, somehow they keep shrinken' away. An' the lovely fruit an' things! An' all that money! O Dil, we know now how rich folks feel, only they're rich all their lives, and we was rich jest that little while. But it was splendid! Rich folks oughter be happy every minnit, an'—an' good. 'Twould be so easy when you lived in a big, beautiful house, an' had flowers an' nice things to eat an' to wear, an' a kerrige to ride in—"

She stopped exhausted, but her eyes glowed with the vision, and a rapture illumined her wan face. Ah, Bess, one poor, forlorn creature, born in the brain of the finest genius of his time, made the same pathetic outcry in her pitiful plight, brought about by her own ill-doing. And you both touched the boundary of a broad truth.

Dil gave a long, quivering breath, and it seemed as if her arms could never unclose again, so tight and fast did they hold their treasure.

"I'm *most* sure he'll come." Bess made a strenuous effort to keep the doubt out of her tone. "He was ter bring the book, you know, and the picture; an' he didn't look 's though he was one of the forgettin' kind. There's somethin'—I can't quite make it out; but Dil, when things is all still, most towards mornin', seems *if* I could hear him talk. Only—it's so long to spring. I'm most sorry we didn't start that day. Why, we might have been to heaven before real cold weather. I'm so tired. Dil, dear, lay me down on the lounge, won't you? It'll rest me a bit."

She put her down softly, and tucked the faded quilt about her. Mamie had fallen asleep on the floor, and she laid her on her own little pallet. The other baby had found a dropped-out knot in the floor, and was trying to put his crust of bread down through it.

Dil washed her dishes and tidied up the house. The clothes from the floor above swung on the pulley-line, and helped to shut out even the chilly gray light. Then there was dinner to get for the boys, who went to school quite steadily. Dan wasn't so bad, though; and Owen had been threatened with the reform-school, "where you had to sweep floors and sew on a machine like a gal!" That did not look so inviting as liberty.

What would happen to-night when her mother came home? Would she, could she, send Bess away?

"'Tain't no use to pray," she thought despairingly within her much-tried soul. "I uster pray about Bess's poor little legs, an' they never mended any. An' mebbe he thought we'd be a bother, an' he'd rather go to heaven alone."

What had become of John Travis?

V—A SONG IN THE NIGHT

In the twenty-four years of John Travis's life he had not done much but please himself. There was never any special pinch in the Travis household, any choice of two things, with the other to be given up entirely. His father was an easy-going man, his mother an amiable society woman, proud, of course, of her good birth. As I said before, excesses were not to John's taste. He didn't look like a fastidious young fellow, but the Travises were clean, wholesome people. Perhaps this was where their good blood really showed itself.

Mr. Travis had a little leaning toward the law for his son; the young fellow fancied he had a little leaning toward medicine. He dallied somewhat with both; he wrote a few pretty society verses; he etched very successfully, and he painted a few pictures, which roused an art ambition within him. He fell in love with a sweet girl in the winter, and in the late summer they had quarrelled and gone separate ways.

There had been another factor in his life,—his cousin, Austin Travis, some twelve years older than himself, his father's eldest brother's only child, and the eldest grandson. Travis farm had been his early home; and there John, the little boy, had fallen in love with the big boy.

Austin was one of the charming society men that women delight in. Every winter girls tried their best for him; and John was made much of on his account, for they were almost inseparable. It was Austin who soothed his uncle's disappointment in the law business. It was Austin who compelled the rather dilatory young fellow to paint in earnest.

Austin had planned a September tour. They would spend a few days with grandmother, and then go to the Adirondacks. He knew a camping-out party of artists and designers that it would be an advantage for John to meet.

John had packed his traps and sent them down to the boat, that was to go out at six. There was nothing special to do. He would walk down, and presently stop in at Brentano's, then take the car. He was very fond of seeing people group themselves together and change like a kaleidoscope. But his heart was sore and indignant, and then his quick eye fell on the withered rose-buds in the shrunken hand of the child, and after that adventure he had barely time to catch his boat.

He hardly knew himself as he sat on the deck till past midnight. Two little poverty-stricken waifs had somehow changed his thoughts, his life. When he was a little boy at Travis Farm a great many curious ideas about heaven had floated through his brain. And when his grandmother sang in her soft, limpid voice,—

"There is a land of pure delight,
Where saints immortal reign;
Infinite day excludes the night,
And pleasures banish pain,"

he used to see it all as a vision. Perhaps his ideas were not much wiser than those of poor little ignorant Bess. He had travelled with Pilgrim; he had known all the people on the way, and they were real enough to him at that period.

Oh, how long ago that seemed! Everything had changed since then. Science had uprooted simple faith. One lived by sight now. The old myths were still beautiful, of course. But long before Christ came, the Greek philosophers had prayed, and the Indian religions had had their self-denying saviours.

But he had promised to find the way to heaven for them, and they were so ignorant. He had promised to go thither himself, and he had dipped into so many philosophies; he knew so much, and yet he was so ignorant. But there must be a heaven, that was one fact; and there must be a way to go thither.

Sunday morning he was in Albany with Austin and two young men he had known through the winter. One of them was very attentive to a pretty cousin who would be found at Travis Farm. They had a leisurely elegant breakfast, they took a carriage and drove about to points of interest, had a course dinner, smoked and talked in the evening. But the inner John was a little boy again, and had gone to church with his grandmother. The sermon was long, and he did not understand it; but he read the hymns he liked, and chewed a bit of fennel, and went almost asleep. The singing was delightful, the spirited old "Coronation."

They went out to Travis Farm the next morning. There was grandmother and Aunt Maria, the single Miss Travis, Daisy Brockholst and her dear friend Katharine Lee. Of course the young people had a good time. They always did at Travis Farm, and they were fond of coming.

"Grandmother," John said, in a hesitating sort of way, "you used to sing an old hymn I liked so much,"

"There is a land of pure delight."

"Have you forgotten it? I wish you would sing it for me," and his hand slipped over hers.

"Why—yes, dear. I go singing about the house for company when no one is here; but old voices are apt to get thin in places, you know."

He did not say he had hunted up an old hymn-book, and read the words over and over. He was ashamed that the children's talk had taken such hold of him. But presently he joined in, keeping his really fine tenor voice down to a low key, and they sang together.

Then there was the soft silence of a country afternoon—the hushed sweetness of innumerable voices that are always telling of God's wonders.

"John," she said, in her low, caressing sort of tone that she had kept from girlhood, "I think heaven won't be quite perfect to me until I hear your voice among the multitude no man can number."

That was all. She had let her life of seventy-four years do her preaching. But she still prayed for her sheaves.

How had he come to have so much courage on Saturday afternoon, and so little now? Of course he could not be *quite* sure. And there would be Austin's incredulous laugh.

They went on to the Adirondacks. He made a sketch of Bess, and sent it to a photographer's with instructions. He was delighted with the artist group. He was planning out his winter. He would take a studio with some one. He would see what he could do for the Quinn children, and paint his fine picture. *She* would see it when it was exhibited somewhere. There would be a curious satisfaction in it. And yet he was carrying around with him every day three faded, shrivelled wild-rose buds.

And then one day they brought in Austin Travis insensible—dead, maybe. There was a little blood stain on his face and his golden brown beard; and it was an hour before they could restore him to consciousness. Just by a miracle he had been saved. A bit of rock that seemed so secure, had been secure for centuries perhaps, split off, taking him down with it. He had the presence of mind to throw away his gun, but the fall had knocked him insensible. He had lain some time before the others found him. There were bruises, a dislocated shoulder, and three broken ribs. Surgery could soon mend those. But there was a puncture in the magnificent lungs, such a little thing to change all one's life; and at first he rebelled with a giant's strength. Life was so much to him, *all* to him. He could *not* go down into nothingness with his days but half told.

Out of all the plans and advice it was settled to try the south of France, and perhaps the Madeira Isles, to take such good care and have such an equable climate that the wound might heal. And John was to be his companion and nurse and friend for all the lighter offices. Austin had hardly allowed him to go out of his sight.

They had returned to New York. Everything was arranged. Austin was impatient to be off before cold weather. For three days John never had a moment; but Bess and Dil had not been out of his mind, and he could steal this afternoon; so, with book and picture, he set out for Barker's Court, not much clearer about the way to heaven than he had been six weeks before.

Barker's Court was not inviting to-day, with its piles of garbage, and wet clothes hanging about like so many miserable ghosts.

"Is it Misses Quinn ye want, or old Granny Quinn?" queried the woman he questioned. "Granny lives up to th' end, an' Misses Quinn's is the third house, up-stairs."

It was semi-twilight. He picked his way up and knocked gently.

So gently, Dil was sure of a customer for her mother. The babies were asleep. Bess was fixed in her wagon. Dil had some patches of bright colors that she was going to sew together, and make a new carriage rug.

She opened the door just a little way. He pushed it wider, and glanced in.

"Oh, have you forgotten me?" he exclaimed. "Did you think I would not come?"

Dil stood in a strange, sweet, guilty abasement. She had disbelieved him. Bess gave a soft, thrilling cry of delight, and stretched out her hands.

"I knew you would come," and there was a tremulous exaltation in her weak voice.

"I've only been in town a few days. I have been staying with a cousin who met with a sad accident and is still ill. But I have run away for an hour or two; and I have brought Bess's picture."

He was taking a little survey of the room. The stove shone. The floor was clean. The white curtain made a light spot in the half gloom. The warmth felt grateful, coming out of the chilly air, though it was rather close. Dil did not look as well as on the summer day. Her eyes were heavy, with purple shadows underneath; the "bang" of the morning had left some traces. And Bess was wasted to a still frailer wraith, if such a thing was possible.

They both looked up eagerly, as he untied the package, and slipped out of an envelope a delicately tinted photograph.

"There, blue eyes, will it do for Dil?"

The child gave a rapturous cry. Dil stood helpless from astonishment.

"There ain't no words good enough," Dil said brokenly. "Leastways, I don't know any. O Bess, he's made you look jes' 's if you was well. O mister, will she look that way in heaven?" For Dil had a vague misgiving she could never look that way on earth.

"She will be more beautiful, because she will never be ill again."

"Dil's right—there ain't no words to praise it," Bess said simply. "If we was rich we'd give you hundreds and hundreds of dollars, wouldn't we, Dil?"

Dil nodded. Her eyes were full of tears. Something she had never known before struggled within her, and almost rent her soul.

"And here is your book. You can read, of course?"

"I can read some. Oh, how good you are to remember." She was deeply conscience stricken.

The tone moved him immeasurably. His eyelids quivered. There were thousands of poor children in the world, some much worse off than these. He could not minister to all of them, but he did wish he could put these two in a different home.

"I must go away again with my cousin, and I am sorry. I meant to"—what could he do, he wondered—"to see more of you this winter; but a friend of mine will visit you, and bring you a little gift now and then. You must have spent all your money long ago," flushing at the thought of the paltry sum.

"We stretched it a good deal," said Dil quaintly. "You see, I bought Bess some clo'es, there didn't seem much comin' in for her. An' the fruit was so lovely. She's been so meachin'."

"Well, I am going to be—did you ever read Cinderella?" he asked eagerly.

"I ain't had much time for readin', an' Bess couldn't go to school but such a little while."

"And no one has told you the story?"

There was a curious eagerness in the sort of blank surprise.

"Well, this little Cinderella did kitchen work; and sat in the chimney-corner when her work was done, while her sisters dressed themselves up fine and went to parties. One evening a curious old woman came, a fairy godmother, and touched her with a wand, a queer little stick she always carried, and turned her old rags into silks and satins, and made a chariot for her, and sent her to the ball at the king's palace."

"Oh," interposed Dil breathlessly, "she didn't have to come back to her rags, an' chimney, an' all, did she?"

"She did come back, because her fairy godmother told her to. But the king's son sent for her and married her."

"Oh, if she'd only come to us, Dil!" Bess had a quicker and more vivid imagination. She had not been so hard worked, nor had her head banged so many times. "We'd have the char—what did you call it? an' go to heaven. Then you wouldn't have to wheel me, Dil, an' we'd get along so much faster." She laughed with a glad, happy softness, and her little face was alight with joy. "Say, mister, you must think I've got heaven on the brain. But if you'd had hurted legs so long, you'd want to get to the Lord Jesus an' have 'em made well. I keep thinkin' over what you told us 'bout your Lord Jesus, an' I know it's true because you've come back."

Such a little thing; such great faith! And he had been comparing claims, discrepancies, and wondering, questioning, afraid to believe a delusion. Was he truly *his* Lord Jesus? The simple belief of the children touched, melted him. It was like finding a rare and exquisite blossom in an arid desert. He wished he were not going away. He would like to care for little Bess until the time of her release came. Ah, would they be disillusioned when they came to know what the real pilgrimage was?

"There ain't no fairies truly," said Dil with pathetic gravity. "There ain't much of anything for poor people."

"I can't take you to a palace; but when I come back I mean you shall have a nice, comfortable home in a prettier place—"

"Mother wouldn't let Dil go on 'count of the babies. There ain't but two to-day, 'n' she was awful mad! 'N' I wouldn't go athout Dil. No one else 'd know how to take care of me."

"We will have that all right. And while I am gone you must have some money to buy medicines and the little luxuries your mother cannot afford."

"She don't buy nothin' ever. I ain't no good, 'cause I'll never walk, 'n' only Dil cares about me," Bess said, as if she had so long accepted the fact the sting was blunted.

"Yes, I care; and I will send a friend here to see you, a young lady, and you need not be afraid to tell her of whatever you want. And Dil may like to know —that I am going to put her in a picture, and the money will be truly her own."

46

He was not sure how much pride or personal delicacy people of this class possessed.

"O Dil!" Bess was electrified with joy. "Oh, I hope you made Dil look—just as she'd look if we lived in one of them beautiful houses, 'n' had a maid 'n' pretty clo'es, 'n' no babies to take care of. We never knowed any one like you afore. Patsey's awful good to us, but he ain't fine like an' soft spoken. Are you very rich, mister?"

He laughed.

"Only middling, but rich enough to make life a little pleasanter for you when I come back."

She seemed to be studying him.

"You look as if you lived in some of the fine, big houses. I'd like to go in wan. An' you know so much! You must have been to school a good deal. Oh, how soft your hands are!"

She laughed delightedly as she enclosed one in both of hers, and then pressed it to her cheek.

He stooped and kissed her. No one ever did that but Dil and Patsey.

"You'll surely come back in time to go to heaven, soon as it's pleasant weather," she said suddenly. "An' Dil couldn't be leaved behind. Mother threatens to put her in a shop, an' she does bang her head cruel. But I wouldn't want to be in a pallis an' have everything, if I couldn't have Dil. An' you'll get it all fixed so's we can go?"

Ah, ah! before that time Bess would have been folded in the everlasting arms. There was a lump in his throat, and he began to untie the string of the book to evade a more decisive answer.

It was an illustrated edition, simplified for children's reading. He turned some of the leaves and found one picture—Christiana ascending the palace steps amid a host of angels.

From this squalid place and poverty, to that—how could he explain the steps between? When he came back Bess would be gone—

"Past night, past day,"

and he would give Dil a new and better chance in spite of her mother.

Dil drew a long, long breath.

"Can we all get to the pallis?" she asked, with a soft awe in her tone.

"Yes, there are many things to do—you will see what Christiana and Mercy did. And if you love the Lord Jesus and pray to him—"

Poor Dil was again conscience smitten. Only this morning she had said praying wasn't any good. She glanced up through tears,—

"'Pears as if I couldn't ever get to understand. I wasn't smart at school—"

"But you *are* smart," interposed Bess. "An' now we've got the book we'll find just how Christiana went. There's only six months left. You'll surely be back by April?"

"I shall be back." His heart smote him. He was a coward after all. Ah, could he ever undertake any of the Master's business?

"Do you remember a hymn an old lady sang for you once?" he said, glad of even this faltering way out. "I have been learning the words."

"'Bout everlasting spring?" and Bess's eyes were alight. "Oh, do please sing it! I'm in such an awful hurry for spring to come. Sometimes my breath gets so short, as if I reely couldn't wait."

Dil raised her eyes with a slow, beseeching movement. He pushed a chair beside the wagon, and held Bess's small hands, that were full of leaping pulses.

The sweet old hymn, almost forgotten amid the clash of modern music. Ah, there was some one who would love and care for Dil in her desolation—his grandmother. He would write to her. Then he began, and at the first note the children were enraptured:—

"There is a land of pure delight,
    Where saints immortal reign;
    Infinite day excludes the night,
    And pleasures banish pain.

Oh, the transporting, rapturous scene,
    That dawns upon my sight;
    Sweet fields arrayed in living green,
    And rivers of delight.

There everlasting spring abides,
    And never-withering flowers;
    Death, like a narrow sea, divides
    This heavenly land from ours.

No chilling winds nor poisonous breath
    Can reach that blessed shore;

Sickness and sorrow, pain and death,
Are felt and feared no more.

O'er all those wide extended plains,
Shines one eternal day;
There Christ the Son forever reigns,
And scatters night away.

Filled with delight, my raptured soul
Can here no longer stay;
Though Jordan's waves around me roll,
Fearless I launch away."

John Travis had a tender, sympathetic voice. Just now he was more moved by emotion than he would have imagined. Dil turned her face away and picked up the tears with her fingers. It was too beautiful to cry about, for crying was associated with sorrow or pain. A great inarticulate desire thrilled through her, a blind, passionate longing for a better, higher life, as if she belonged somewhere else. And, like Bess, an impatience pervaded her to be gone at once.

"Oh, please do sing it again!" besought Bess in a transport, her face spiritualized to a seraphic beauty. "Did they sing like that in the Mission School, Dil?"

Dil shook her head in speechless ecstasy.

There was a knock, and then the door opened softly. It was Mrs. Murphy, with her sick baby in her arms.

"Ah, dear," she began deprecatingly, with an odd little old country courtesy, "I heard the singing, an' I said to poor old Mis' Bolan, 'That's never the Salvation Army, for they do make such a hullabaloo; but it must be a Moody an' Sankey man that I wunst haird, with the v'ice of an angel.' An' the pore craythur is a hankerin' to get nearer. Will ye lit her come down, plaise, or will ye come up?"

John Travis flushed suddenly. Dil glanced at her visitor aghast. Some finer instinct questioned whether he were offended. But he smiled. If it would give a poor old woman a pleasure—

Dil was considering a critical point. She had learned to be wise in evading the fury of a half-drunken woman. There were many things she kept to herself. But Mrs. Murphy would talk *him* over. A Moody and Sankey man,—she had not a very clear idea; but if Mrs. Murphy knew, it might be wisdom to have some one here who would speak a good word for her if it should be needed.

"Ye can bring her down," she answered, still looking at John Travis with rising color.

She simply stepped into the hall; but the old woman was half-way downstairs, and needed no further summons.

"Ah, dear, it's the v'ice of an angel shure. An' though I'm not given to them kind of maytins, on account of the praist, they do be beautiful an' comfortin' whiles they sing. Come in. It's Dilly Quinn that'll bid ye welcome. For it's the Moody an' Sankey man."

"Yer very good, Dilly Quinn, very good, to ask in a poor old woman; though I'm main afeared of yer mother in a tantrum." Her voice was shrill and shaky, though she was not seventy; but poverty and hardships age people fast. A bowed and shrunken woman, with thin, white, straggling hair, watery, hungry-looking eyes, a wrinkled, ashen skin, her lips a leaden blue and sunken from lack of teeth. She had one of Mrs. Murphy's rooms since the head of the house was safely bestowed within prison limits. Mrs. Bolan's only son had been killed in the war, and she had her pension. Now and then some one gave her a little work out of pity.

She dropped down on the lounge. "When I heard that there hymn," she went on quaveringly, "it took me back forty year an' more. There was great revival meetin's. My poor old mother used to sing it. But meetin's don't seem the same any more, or else we old folks kinder lost the end er r'ligion."

She was so pitiful, with her timorous, lonely look, and the hard struggles time had written on her everywhere.

"Will you sing it for her?" Dil asked timidly, glancing up at Travis.

Some one else paused to listen and look in, and stared with strange interest at the fine young fellow, whose rich, deep voice found a way to their hearts. And as he sang, a realization of their pinched, joyless lives filled him with dismay. Mrs. Bolan rocked herself too and fro, her hands clutched tightly over her breast, as if she was hugging some comfort she could not afford to let go. The tears rolled silently down her furrowed cheeks.

The foreign part of the audience was more outspoken.

"Ah, did yez iver listen to the loikes! Shure, it would move the heart of a sthone. It's enough to take yez right t'ro' to heaven widout the laste taste o' purgatory. Shure, Mrs. Kelly, it's like a pack o' troubles fallin' off, an' ye step out light an' strong to yer work agen. There'll be a blissin' for ye, young man, for the pleasure ye've given."

Mrs. Bolan shuffled forward and caught his hand in hers, which seemed almost to rattle, they were so bony.

"God bless you, sir." Her voice was so broken it sounded like sobs. "An' there's something 'bout makin' his face shine on you—I disremember, it's so long since I've read my Bible, more shame to me; but my eyes are so old and bad, I hope the Lord won't lay it up agen me. I'm a poor old body, pushed outen the ranks. And you get kicked aside. Ye see, 'tain't every voice that takes one to heaven. Lord help us 'bout gettin' in. But mebbe he'll be merciful to all who go astray. An'—if ye wouldn't mind sayin' a bit of prayer, 'pears like 'twould comfort me to my dyin' day."

Her hungry eyes pleaded through their tears.

A bit of prayer! He had been praying a little for himself of late, but it came awkward after his years of intellectual complacency. A youngish woman was glancing at him in frightened desperation, as if she waited for something to turn her very life. There was but one thing he could think of in this stress— the divine mandate. Could anything be more complete? When ye pray, say,—

"Our Father which art in heaven—"

VI—A WONDERFUL STORY

John Travis stood with upraised hand. Clearly, slowly, the words fell, and you could hear only the labored respiration of the women. There was a benediction—he could not recall it, but a verse of Scripture came into his mind. *"Peace I leave with you, my peace I give unto you: not as the world giveth give I unto you. Let not your heart be troubled, neither let it be afraid."*

"The Lord will bless you," said the trembling old woman.

He squeezed something into her hand as she turned to go. Mrs. Murphy's sickly baby began to cry, and one of Dil's woke up. The little crowd dispersed.

It began to grow dusky. Night came on early in Barker's Court. Days were shorter, and sunless at that.

Travis stepped back to Bess.

"I shall ask my friend to tell me all about you—she will write it. And I shall come back." He stooped and kissed Bess on the brow, for the last time. Heaven help her on her lonely journey. But the Saviour who blessed little children would be tender of her surely.

"We'll all go—won't we—to heaven? The singin' was so beautiful. An' the everlastin' spring."

"Good-by." He clasped Dil's hand. "Remember, wherever you are, I shall find you. Oh, do not be afraid, God will care for you."

"I don't seem to understand 'bout God," and there was a great, strange awe in Dil's eyes. "But you've been lovely. I can understand that."

One more glance at Bess, whose face was lighted with an exalted glow, as if she were poised, just ready for flight. Oh, what could comfort Dil when she was gone? And *he* had so much! He was so rich in home and love.

A woman stood in the lower hallway, the half-despairing face he had noted. She clutched his arm.

"See here," she cried. "You said, 'deliver us from evil.' Is anybody—is God strong enough to do it? From horrible evil—when there seems no other way open—when you must see some one you love—die starvin'—an' no work to be had—O my God!"

The cry pierced him. Yes, there was a beneficent power in money. He gave thanks for it, as he crushed it in her hand. How did the poor souls live, herded in this narrow court? His father's stable was a palace to it in cleanliness.

He had reasoned about poverty being one of the judicious forces of the world. He had studied its picturesque aspects, its freedom from care and responsibility, its comfortable disregard of conventionals, its happy indifference to custom and opinion. Did these people look joyous and content? Why, their faces even now haunted him with the weight of hopeless sorrow. Oh, what could he do to ease the burthen of the world?

Dil picked up the baby after she had lighted the lamp. She was still in a maze, as if some vision had come and gone. Was he really here? Or had she been in a blissful dream?

"Come an' spell out what he's written—an'—an' his name, Dil!"

Bess was studying the fly-leaf. Yes, there it was, "John Travis."

"I wisht it wasn't John," said Bess, a little disappointed. "He ought to have a fine, grand name, he's so splendid. Rich people have nice ways, that poor people can't seem to get."

"No, they can't get 'em, they can't," Dil repeated, with a despairing sense of the gulf between. She had never thought much about rich people before.

"You'd better hide the book, an' the money, 'fore Owny comes in," said Bess fearfully. "I don't even dast to look at the pictures. But we'll have it a good many days when mammy's out, an' I must learn to read the hard words. O Dil! if I had two good legs, I would jump for joy."

Dil wanted to sit down and cry from some unknown excess of feeling—she never had time to cry from pure joy. But she heeded Bess's admonition, and hid their precious gifts. Then she stirred the fire and put on the potatoes. It was beginning to rain, and the boys came in noisily. The babies went home, and they had supper.

It was quite late when Mrs. Quinn returned home, and she threw a bundle on the lounge. The boys being in, and Bess out of the way, she had nothing to scold about. She had had her day's work praised, and a good supper in the bargain. Then cook had given her a "drap of the craythur" to keep out the cold. And she could have two days' work every week "stiddy," so she resolved to throw over some poorer customer.

But when Mrs. Murphy came down with a few potatoes in her hand that she had borrowed, and full of her wonderful news, Dil's heart sank within her like lead.

"An' what do ye think?" the visitor began incautiously. "Poor old Mrs. Bolan is half wild with all the singin' an' the beautiful prisint he gev her."

"What prisint?" asked Mrs. Quinn peremptorily.

"Why, it was a five-dollar bill. I thought first she'd faint clear away wid joy."

"What man?" eying them both suspiciously.

Dil's lips moved, but her throat was so dry she could not utter a sound.

"Wan of them Moody an' Sankey men that do be singin' around, an' prayin'. An' ye niver heard sich an' iligant v'ice even at the free and easies! Why, Mrs. Quinn, it's my belafe, in spite of the praist, he cud draw a soul out o' purgatory just wid his singin'. Mrs. Bolan's that 'raptured she does nothin' but quaver about wid her shaky old v'ice. Ah, dear—ave ye cud hev heard him!"

"To the divil wid him! Comin' round to git money out'v poor folks. I knows 'em. Dil, did you give him a cint?"

"I didn't have any; but he didn't ast for none," and the poor child had hard work to steady her voice.

"An' ye'r mistaken, Mrs. Quinn, if ye think the likes of sich a gentleman would be beggin' of the poor," returned Mrs. Murphy indignantly. "An' he a-gevin a poor ould craythur five dollars! An' they do be goin' around a-missionin' with their prayers and hymns."

"I know 'em. An' the praists an' the sisters beggin' the last cint, an' promisin' to pray ye outen purgatory! Mrs. Murphy," with withering contempt, "them men cuddent pray ye outen a sewer ditch if ye fell in! An' I won't have them comin' here—ye hear that, Dilsey Quinn! If I catch a Moody an' Sankey man here, I'll break ivery bone in his body, an' yours too; ye hear that now!"

Mrs. Quinn was evidently "spilin'" for a fight." Mrs. Murphy went off in high dudgeon without another word.

But she stopped to pour out her grievance to Mrs. Garrick on her floor.

"Shure, I pity them childers, for their mother do be the worst haythen an' infidel, not belayvin' a word about her own sowl, an' spindin' her money for gin as she do. She was a foine-lukin' woman, an' now her eyes is all swelled up, an' her nose the color of an ould toper. An' that poor little Bess dyin' afore her very eyes widout a bit of a mass, or even christenin' I belayve. I'm not that bigoted, Mrs. Garrick, though the praists do say there bees but the wan way. I'm willin' that people shall try their own ways, so long as they save their sowls; but pore, helpless bits of childer that can't know! An' what are their mothers put in the wurruld for but to tache them? But when ye don't belayve ye have a sowl of yer own it's awful! There's them b'ys runnin' wild —an' a moighty good thing it'll be whin they're in the 'form-school, kapin' out o' jail, an' wuss!"

Dil sat in awful fear when the door had closed behind their neighbor. She took up Owen's trousers—the rent was sufficient to send any boy early to bed.

That recalled her mother. She threw the bundle towards Dil.

"There's some clo'es ye kin be fixin' up for Dan, whin ye've so much time as to be spindin' it on Moody and Sankey men, drat 'em! foolin' 'round an' wastin' valyble time. Next I'll hear that ye've ast in the organ man an' the monkey, and I'll come home to find ye givin' a pairty. An' ye'll hev yer head broke for it, that ye will!"

So long as it was not broken now, Dil gave secret thanks. Did God help any? Then, why didn't he help other times when things were very bad? She examined the suit, and found it a nice one, rather large for Dan, who was not growing like a weed, although he ran the streets.

Her mother began to snore. She would be good for some hours' sound sleep. So Dil stole into the little room, and began to prepare Bess for bed, though she trembled with a half fear.

"O Dil, I didn't hardly dast to breathe! An' if she'd known *he* come in here an' sung, she'd murdered us! An' it made me feel glad like that he was goin' away, for mammy might happen to be home when he come—though don't you b'lieve he'd take us away right then? An'—an'wasn't it lucky you didn't have to tell about the—"

Bess held the bill up in her hand.

"Le's put it in the book, an' hide the book in the bottom of the wagon. An', Dil, I can't help feeling light like, as if I was goin' to float. Think of that splendid place, an' no night, an' no winter, an' all beautiful things. Oh, I wisht he'd gev us the words too; I'm most sure I could sing 'em. An' the best of all is that mammy won't be there, cause, you see, 'twouldn't please her any, and I'd be awful feared. She'd ruther stay here an' drink gin."

They had not gone far enough in the Christian life, poor ignorant little souls, to have much missionary spirit. But they kissed, and kissed softly, in the half-dark, and cried a little—tender tears touched with a sadness that was as sweet as joy.

Dil stepped about cautiously, emptied the grate, and did up her night-work. There seemed a certainty about heaven that she had not experienced before, a confidence in John Travis that gave her a stubborn faith. He would surely return in the spring. They would go out some day and never, never come back to Barker's Court.

She fell asleep in her visionary journey when she was up beyond Central Park. She was always so tired, and this night quite exhausted. But Bess kept floating on a sea of delicious sound; and if ever one had visions of the promised land, it was Bessy Quinn.

There were seven babies in the next morning, it being a sharp, clear day. Mrs. Quinn had gone off about her business with no row. When Bess had been dressed and had her breakfast, they drew out the precious book.

"I'll jes' cover it with a bit of old calico an' no one will mistrust, for you can jes' slip it down in the carriage. An' we'll get out that old speller of Owny's, so mother can see that around if we do be taken by s'prise."

They looked at the pictures as the babies would allow them the leisure, and spelled out the explanation underneath. It was so wonderful, though at times they were appalled by the difficulties and dangers. And it was almost night when they reached the crowning-point of all,—Christiana going across the river.

"All the banks beyond the river were full of horses and chariots which were come down from above to accompany her to the City Gate." Her friends were thronging round. She was entering the river with a fearless step and uplifted face.

"Why, Dil, she jes' walked right acrost." Bess gave a joyous little laugh. "You see, she couldn't get drownded, because that Lord Jesus had made it all right an' safe, jes' as he carried people in his arms. I'm so glad we know. You see, when we get to the river, an' it will be way, way above Cent'l Park, when we've been through these giants an' all—an' I'm *most* afraid of thim; but the man did not let 'em hurt her, an' *he*, our man, won't let 'em hurt us. An' we'll jest step right in the river,—maybe *he'll* carry me acrost on account of my poor little legs,—an' we sha'n't be a mite afraid, for he won't let us drown. O Dil, it'll be so lovely! An' here's the pallis!"

There was the "throng that no man can number," welcoming Christiana. Angels with spreading wings and rapturous faces. Her husband coming to meet her, and the Lord Jesus ministering an abundant welcome.

What a day it was! Never was day so short, so utterly delightful. Some of the babies were cross: out of seven little poorly born and poorly nourished babies, there were wants and woes; but Dil hugged them, cuddled them, crooned to them, with a radiant bliss she had never known before. She could look so surely at the end.

An old debt of half a dollar came in, and there were thirty-five cents for the babies. Dan had on his new suit too, and altogether Mrs. Quinn was remarkably good-natured. Dil felt almost conscience-smitten about the book —but then the story would have to come out, and alas!

After that they began to read the wonderful story. Dil was not much of a scholar. Her school-days had been few and far between, never continuous enough to give her any real interest. Indeed, she had not been bright at her books, and her mother had not cared. School was something to fill up the time until children were old enough to go to work. But Dil surely had enough to fill up her time.

Bess would have far outstripped her in learning. But Dil had a shrewd head, and was handy with her needle. She possessed what Yankee people call "faculty;" and her training had given her a sharp lookout for any short cuts in what she had to do, as well as a certain tact in evading or bridging over rough places.

But the reading was very hard labor. They did not know the meaning or the application of words, and their pronouncing ability was indeed halting.

They had not even attained to the practical knowledge acquired by mingling with other children. Dil's life had been pathetic in its solitariness, like the loneliness of a strange crowd. Other children had not "taken to her." Her days had been all work. She would have felt awkward and out of place playing with anything but a baby.

Bess found the most similitudes in Christiana. Even John Travis would have been amused by her literal interpretation. Though it had been simplified for children's reading, it was far above their limited capacity. But the pictures helped so much; and when Dil could not get "the straight of it," when the spiritual part tried and confused their brains, they turned to Christiana crossing the river and entering heaven.

Valiant Mr. Greatheart appealed strongly to Bess.

"He's got such a strong, beautiful name," she declared enthusiastically. "He always comes when there's troubles, an' gettin' lost, an' all that. I 'most wish *his* name was Mr. Greatheart. He could fight, I know; not this common, hateful fightin' down here in the court, but with giants an' wild beasts. An' there were the boys, Dil; but I s'pose Owny wouldn't care 'bout goin'."

"Well," Dil hesitated curiously, "you've got to try to be good some way, an' Owny wouldn't quit swearin' an' snivyin' when he got a chance. An' I don't think he'd understand. Then he might tell mammy 'bout our plans."

"An' mammy jes' wouldn't let you stir a step, I know. An' I couldn't go athout you, Dil, though there'll be many people on the road. I was most feared it would be lonesome like."

"An' I'll be gettin' a few clo'es ready, the best of thim. I'll wash an' iron your new white dress when we don't go out no more, an' put it away kerful. An' I hope some one will give mother some clo'es for a big girl! I'll be so glad to go, for sometimes I'm so tired I jes' want to drop."

"But October's 'most gone. An' last winter don't seem long to me now, an' the summer that was so hot,—but it had that beautiful Sat'day when we found *him*. An' to think of havin' him forever 'n' ever!"

Dil gave a long sigh. She was as impatient as Bess, but she hardly dared set her heart upon the hope.

She was a very busy little woman, and her mind had to be on her work. The garments given to the boys had, of course, the best taken out of them, and Owen was hard on his clothes. As for the stockings, their darning was a work of labor, if not of love. Bess had to be kept warm and comfortable, and Dil tried to make her pretty as well. There were some rainy Saturdays, and the one baby often came in that day. But she tried to give Bess an airing on Sunday. It was such a change for the poor little invalid.

Mrs. Quinn was better pleased to be busy all the time. Besides the money, which was really needed now that fires were more expensive, she liked the change, the gossiping and often it was a pleasure to find fault with her customers. She still went to Mrs. MacBride's of an evening.

With the advent of November came a week of glorious Indian summer weather. And one Saturday Mrs. Quinn was to do some cleaning at a fine house, and stay to help with a grand dinner. Dil rushed through with her work, and they went up to the Square that afternoon, and sat in the old place. The sparrows came and chirped cheerfully; but the flowers were gone, the trees leafless. Yet it was delightful to picture it all again.

John Travis would have felt sorry for Dil to-day—perhaps if he had seen her for the first time he would not have been so instantly attracted. Her eyes were heavy, her skin dark and sodden. Even Bess grew weary with the long ride. But they shopped a little again; and Dil was extravagant enough to buy some long, soft woollen stockings for Bess's "poor, hurted legs."

"I'm so tired," she said afterward. "'Tain't quite like summer, is it? Make up a good fire, Dil, an' get me snappin' warm."

She did not want much to eat. Even the grapes had lost their flavor.

"I wish you could sing that beautiful hymn," she said to Dil. "I'd just like to hear it, 'cause it keeps floatin' round all the time, an' don't get quite near enough. O Dil! don't you s'pose you can sing in heaven?"

"Seems to me I heard at the Mission School that everybody would. If the Lord Jesus can mend your legs, I'm sure he can put some music in my throat."

"We'll ask him right away. Then read to me a little."

Bess fell asleep presently. Dil made slow work spelling out the words and not knowing half the meanings. Her seasons at the Mission School had always been brief, from various causes. Now and then some visitor came in, but the talk was often in phrases that Dil did not understand. She had not a quick comprehension, neither was she an imaginative child.

Looking now at Bess's pinched and pallid face a strange fear entered her mind. Would Bess be strong enough in the spring to take the long journey? For it was so much longer than she imagined, and Bess couldn't be made well until they reached the Lord Jesus. There was a vague misgiving tugging at her heart. They ought to have gone that lovely Saturday.

They talked so much about John Travis that they almost forgot what he had said about his friend. They were husbanding their small resources for the time of need. There had been so many babies that Dil had not needed to make up deficiencies. Sometimes they felt quite afraid of their hiding-place, and Dil made a little bag and put it around Bess's neck, so no one would come upon the money unaware.

The touch of Indian summer was followed by a storm and cool, brisk winds. It was too cold to take Bess out, even if she had cared; but she had been rather drooping all the week. There was a baby in, also, and Bess kept in her own room, as she often did Saturday morning, to be out of the way of her mother's sharp frowns.

Dil had gone of an errand. Mrs. Quinn sat furbishing up an ulster she had bought at a second-hand store at a great bargain. The baby was asleep on the lounge. When Dil returned, a dreadful something met her on the threshold that made her very heart stand still.

"I have come from a Mr. Travis, to see the children. He has gone abroad, and he asked me to look after them."

This was what had gone before—very little, indeed. Mrs. Quinn had answered, "Come in," to a tap at the door; and there had entered a rather pretty, well-dressed, well-bred young woman, who considered herself quite an important member of the charitable world. She saw a clean-looking room with more comforts than usual, and she gave a sharp glance around the corners.

Mrs. Quinn received her very civilly, considering her a possible customer.

"You have a little girl who is an invalid, I believe?" she queried.

"That I have," was the brief reply.

The stranger glanced at the two open doors, and wondered; was the child in bed?

The next sentence was what Dil had caught. Miss Nevins checked herself suddenly. Mr. Travis had said, "See the children alone if you can. Their mother is out to work most of the time, and it will be an easy matter. But do not give any money to the woman for them; they will not get it."

"Well—what?" asked Mrs. Quinn sharply, with an aspect that rather nonplussed the lady. "Whin did he see so much of thim, an' come to think they needed his attintion?"

"Why—when he was here—"

"Was he here now? an' what called him?"

Mrs. Quinn gave her visitor an insolent stare that rendered her very uncomfortable.

"I—I really do not know *when*. Kindly disposed people *do* visit the sick and the needy. I go to a great many places—"

"Av ye plaise," she interrupted, "we're not paupers. I'm well enough, ye see, to be takin' care of me own childers. An' he nor no one else nade throubble theirselves. I'm not askin' charity; an' av they did it unbeknownst to me, I'll hammer thim well, that I will! They're as well off as common folk, an' ye needn't be worritin'. Av that's all ye come fer, ye kin be goin' about yer own bisniss, bedad! An' ye kin tell Mr. What's-his-name that I'm not sufferin' fer help."

This was not the fashion in which Miss Nevins was generally received. "You do not understand"—with rising color. "We desire to be of whatever service we can; and if your child is ill, you cannot have a better friend—"

"Frind! is it? Bedad, I kin choose me own frinds! An' if he knows whin he's well off, he'll not show his foine forrum here, er his mug'll get a party mash on it. Frind, indade!"

The irate woman looked formidable as she rose, but Miss Nevins did not mean to be daunted.

"You may see the time when you will be glad of a friend, though you need not worry about *his* coming. I shall tell him you are not worth his interest. As for the child"—and her indignation sparkled in her eyes.

"The child wants none of his help, ye kin tell him. I kin look afther her mesilf."

"Good-day," and the visitor opened the door. Dil stepped back in the obscurity. The lady held up her fine cloth gown, and gave her nose a haughty wrinkle or two as she inhaled the stifling air once, and then did not breathe until she was in the court.

"Such a horrid hole!" she commented. "The child ought to be moved to a hospital—or perhaps she is well by this time. John is so easily taken in—his swans so often turn out to be geese. As if *I* would have given her any money, the impudent, blowsy thing! I know pretty well how far to trust that class! Though it's rather funny," and she smiled in the midst of her disgust; "they are always whining and pleading poverty, and will be abject enough for a quarter. And she was very high and mighty! I'll write a good long letter to John about it, but I won't trouble her ladyship again."

Dil stood shaking with terror, and some moments elapsed before she had courage enough to open the door. She was in a degree prepared for a line of defence.

Her mother seized her by the arm, and fairly shouted at her,—

"Who was the man who kim to see ye, ye young huzzy?"

"Man! When did a man come? I don't remember," assuming surprise.

"I'll help yer mem'ry thin wid that;" and Dil's ears rang with the sound of the blow.

"There wasn't any man since the wan that sang a long whiles ago. Mrs. Murphy knew. She said he was a Moody an' Sankey man, an' that they do be goin' round singin' and prayin'. An' they all stood in the hall, the women about. Mrs. Murphy kin tell you."

Mrs. Quinn was rather nonplussed.

"What did he gev ye?"

"Nothin'," sobbed Dil. "It was poor old Mrs. Bolan that had the money."

"Not a cint?" She took Dil by the shoulder. "Dil Quinn, I don' no whether to belave yer; but if he'd gev ye any money, an' ye'd bin such a deceivin' little thafe, I'd break ivery bone in yer mean little body. Howld yer tongue! I ain't done nothin' but ast a civil question."

Dil tried to stop sobbing. Her mother was in a hurry to get out, or matters might have been worse.

"Stop yer snivelin'," commanded her mother. "But if I hear of any more men singin' round, I'll make ye wish yer never been born."

The baby cried at this juncture, and Dil took it up. Mrs. Quinn went out, and there would be peace until midnight.

Bess sat in the carriage, wild-eyed and ghostly, trembling in every limb.

"It was a norful lie!" sobbed Dil. "But if I'd told her, she'd killed me! *He* wouldn't a done such a thing; but nobody'd darst to tackle him, an' rich people don't beat an' bang."

"You didn't tell no lie," said Bess in a sudden strong voice. "*He* never gev you no money. 'Twarn't your money 't all. Doncher know he put it in the bag the first time when you was feared to take it, an' he jes' dropped it down here in the side of the kerrige. He never gev you a penny. An' it was *my* money."

"O Bess! Ye'r such a bright, smart little thing! If you'd been well we'd just kept ahead of mother all the time;" and now the sunshine slanted over the brown quartz eyes that were swimming in tears. "I d'n' know, but I should have hated norful to tell a lie 'bout him. He seems—well, I can't somehow git the right words; but's if you wanted to be all on the square when he liked you. I don't b'leve he'd so much mind yer snivyin' out a nickel when there was a good many babies, an' puttin' it back when there wasn't, to save gettin' yer head busted. But he wouldn't tell no lie. He kem when he said he would an' brought Christiana, an' he'll come in the spring, sure."

"Yes, sure," said Bess, with a faint smile. "But you better ast Mrs. Murphy to keep the book a few days, for mammy might go snoopin' about—"

"I just will; but I don't b'leve she'd dast to hustle you round and find the money. An' now a week's gone, an' there's only three left, en then it'll be anuther month, an' O Bess, spring! spring!"

There was an exultant gladness in Dil's voice.

VII—MARTYRED CHRISTIANA.

Dil was always so tired, she went to sleep at once from exhaustion. But to-night every nerve seemed in a quiver. They had found some medicine that soothed Bess and kept her from coughing, so she slept better than in the summer. Dil tossed and tumbled. There had been given her a magnificent endowment of physical strength, and the dull apathy of poverty had kept her from a prodigal waste of nerve force. She was what people often called stolid, but she had never been roused. How many poor souls live and die with most of their energies dormant.

There had never been but one dream to Dil's life, and that was Bess. Here her imagination had some play. When they took their outings through the more respectable streets for the cleanliness and quiet, or paused awhile in the green and flowery squares, she sometimes "made believe" that Bess was the lovely child in the elegant carriage, with wraps of eider down and lace, and she the nurse-maid in white apron and cap who trundled her along jauntily. Or else it was Bess, blue-eyed and golden-haired, sitting in a real "grown-up" carriage with her pretty mamma in silks and satins. The little nurse-maid was at home, putting everything in order, and waiting for the lovely princess to come back and tell her all she had seen. That and heaven had been the extent of her romancing.

But to-night a curious, separate life stirred within her. A consciousness of the great difference between such people as John Travis, even the lady in the hall who had so disdainfully gathered up her skirts and scattered a faint fragrance about. Why was such a great difference made? Why should she and Bess be Honor Quinn's children? Would another mother be given them in heaven?

The mothers in the court seemed to love their little babies, yet afterward they beat and banged them about. But the children in that clean, beautiful world where there was no pain, the children in heaven—ah! ah! She was not crying with human passion; it was the deep anguish of the soul that cannot even find vent in tears, the throes of an awful inward pain, that seldom, thank God, comes to the young, that dense ignorance often keeps from the very poor.

"Took them in his arms." That was what John Travis had said. She was so tired to-night—not the fatigue of hard work altogether, but a great aching that had no name. If she could be taken in some one's arms! Dilsey Quinn could not remember being held, though her mother had been proud of her first-born, and fond too, in those days.

If Mrs. Quinn's life had been a little more prosperous, if she had lived in a cottage with a patch of ground, a cow and some chickens, and the wholesome surroundings of the little village where she had reigned a sort of rural queen, her children might have known love and tenderness. But the babies had come fast. Her man had taken to drink. They were crowded in among the poor and ignorant, where brawls and oaths, drinking and cruelty, were daily food. Ah, what wonder one lapses into barbarism! For the last half-dozen years she had slaved, and sometimes gone hungry. She could have strangled little Dan when he came, for adding to her burthens. How much of the peril of the soul depends upon the surroundings!

And now Dil longed for the strong arms to be about her. Do you wonder she had so little idea of a heavenly Father? The teaching of the Mission School had been measured by the hard, bare materialism of poverty, quite as upas-like as the materialism of philosophy. It had a rather dainty aspect when John Travis dallied with it among his college compeers; but it seems shocking when these hundreds of little children cannot even formulate the idea of a God. And though Dil stretched out her hands with an imploring moan, it was for some present and personal comfort.

Owny came creeping in softly, and just saved his skin, for to-night his mother returned earlier than usual. She was growing stout, and walked solidly. She seemed to be puttering about. Then she pushed Dil's door wide open, and there was barely room for her. The lamp stood on the floor outside. Dil's "chest of drawers" was covered with a curtain of various pieces, and she had ornamented the top with treasures found amid the cast-off Christmas and Easter cards that had fallen to her when more favored children had tired of them. A cigar-box was covered with some bits of silk, and held a few paltry "treasures." Some fancy beads, a tarnished bangle, a bit of ribbon, and so on, she found as she dumped them in her apron and then thrust them back. Next she dragged the articles out of the improvised "drawers," and shook them one by one. Nothing contraband fell out. There was nothing to reward her search, and she glared at the child in the faded, shabby wagon.

Dil hardly breathed. She remembered in that half-frozen, fascinated sort of way that horrible events will rise up, ghost-like, in times of terror—that one night last winter, a woman farther up the court had murdered her two little children, and then killed herself. She was cold with an awful apprehension of evil. Even though she kept her eyes closed, she could seem to see with that awesome, inward sight.

Mrs. Quinn thrust her hand under Bess's pillow, under her bed, and the poor child gave a broken, disturbed half-cry. Her efforts were fruitless; but before Dil could give a sound to her horrible fear, she had turned and was facing her.

Then Dil sprang partly up, but the scream curdled in her throat.

"Oh, ye naydent disturb yersilf this time o' night. I was jist lookin' in upon me two gals that the man was so distrissed about. Dil Quinn, av' ye iver go to the bad like some gals, I'll not lave a square inch of skin on yer body, ner a whole bone inside. I'll have no men singin' round whiles I'm not here. You shut the door on 'em, jist. You're a humbly little runt, God knows, but thim kind is purty hard whin they once set out. Ye mind, now! An' that un—"

She shook her fist, and backed out of the room, for she could hardly have turned around. Bess moaned, but she was not awake. Dil used all her strength to suppress a scream, while a cold perspiration oozed from every pore.

When she dared, after the lamp was out, she rose and changed Bess to a more comfortable position. Ah, if the book had been there! The child shuddered with vague apprehension.

All the rest of the night she lay fearfully awake, and the next morning she looked ghastly. Even her mother was moved.

"You don't look well, Dil," she said. "What's got yer?"

"My head aches." Had she dreamed that horrible vision of the night?

"Take some queuann. Ye've no toime to be sick. Ye spind too much toime over the brat there. An' it'll be a mercy whin it's all over. I cuddent stan' it mesilf much longer."

Patsey came that afternoon. Business was good, and he had a few dimes in the bank. He and three other boys boarded with an old woman.

"But I've been thinkin', Dil, that if we had you instid o' the old woman! She can't make an Irish stew worth shucks, an' yers wud jist make a felly sing in his sleep. Whin I git some money ahead I'll jist have youse come. Yer mammy'll not mind if ye take Bess."

Dil smiled. It was lovely of Patsey, but they would be going to heaven then. She wondered why they didn't care to take Patsey along when they were so fond of him. He wouldn't want to go—how she knew that she could not tell, either.

He brought Bess a splendid orange and some candy and an illustrated paper. The pictures were very entertaining.

"Bess is lookin' slim," he said. "She wants to go out in the fresh air."

"But it's so cold, an' it just goes over me an' all through, as if I hadn't half enough clo'es on. No, I must stay in an' keep good an' warm, an' get well by spring."

"That's the talk," and Patsey smiled.

When he was gone and they were all alone, they looked at each other curiously.

"'Twould be nice to go an' live with Patsey if we wasn't goin' to heaven," Bess said. "I do be so afeard of mammy sometimes."

"An' she rummiged last night, Bess, on the shelves an' in your bed; an' if it hadn't been for yer wit she'd a found the book. I was so glad it was in Misses Murphy's, an' I guess I'll keep it up there every night; an' if she finds out an' asts, I'll say an' old trac'woman left it. She won't mind an old woman. I sh'd hate to tell such a lie, but when we see *him* we'll tell him how it was. 'Cause we can't be murdered."

"We just won't tell any one 'bout goin' to heaven, either. Only Patsey, just at the last."

Mrs. Quinn dropped her suspicions in a few days. The weather was growing colder, and she needed a little more to keep up the internal fires. She managed to pay her rent promptly, and so had a good reputation with the agent. Through Dil's good management the boys fared very well as to food, but Bess did not eat enough to keep a bird alive.

"But the medicine helps," she said. "It's such splendid medicine! so much better'n that 'Spensary stuff."

The morphine in it soothed and quieted. Sometimes Bess slept all the morning, and now she was seldom wakeful at night. Dil thought that an improvement. If only she was not so frightfully thin!

The days sped on with little variation. At Thanksgiving they had two turkeys, and several of Mrs. Quinn's cronies came in to dinner. They feasted all the rest of the week.

And now another month was gone. Only four remained.

Alas! with all their care and caution, and the ready sympathy of Mrs. Murphy, there came a swift, crushing martyrdom to their much-loved Christiana, almost to Dil. She had hurried her supper dishes out of the way, tidied up the room, and, as her mother had gone to Mrs. MacBride's, Dan in bed with a cold, and Owen roaming the streets, Dil brought out her book for an hour's reading. They had come to Giant Grim and his blustering threats to the Pilgrims, who would have fared badly indeed but for Mr. Greatheart. Dil had to stop to spell many of the words; often it took the united efforts of both brains to decide the meaning of a sentence.

The door opened, and Mrs. Quinn walked in. There had been a rather heated talk at Mrs. MacBride's.

Dil paused suddenly, with a swift, startled breath.

"What's that ye got?" She came nearer and glared over Dil. "An' who gev ye that?"

"A—a woman left it!" exclaimed Dil tremulously. "An old woman with trac's —"

She pulled Dil up to her feet, and the book fell to the floor.

"An' it wasn't that—that singin' man?"

She shook her so that Dil could scarcely make a sound, and for once she hardly minded.

"No man has been here," declared Bess.

"Shet yer head!" roared her mother. "Pick up that buke. What's it all about?"

"'Bout a woman they told me of in the Mission School. She took her children an'—was goin' to heaven—"

"Well, you've got business here, an' ye'll be tindin' to it, it's my opinion. Ye ain't got time for no sich foolin'. Yer wurruk will kape ye busy. Ye best not be settin' up fer a schollard. The radin' an' the stuff'll turn your head upside down. Take that!"

Mrs. Quinn gave her a resounding blow with it. Before Dil could fairly see, she had marched over to the stove.

"O mother! mother!" shrieked Dil as she caught her arm.

Mrs. Quinn gave her a push that sent her staggering across the room. She raised the stove-lid, and crowded in the book.

"Ye'll not waste yer time over any sich nonsense. Git off to bed at wanst, er I'll make ye see stars! Take that measlin' brat along wid ye."

Dil turned the wagon into the small chamber without another word. Bess caught her hands, but neither dared speak.

"Where's Owny?" the mother demanded.

"I don't know," almost sobbed Dil.

"I'll not hev him runnin' the streets at night! A foine sister yes are, to be sure, readin' novils, an' lettin' yer pore brother go to destruction! If ye don't kape him in at night I'll know the reason why. I'll lie here a bit, an' I'll give him a norful larrupin' when he comes."

Mrs. Quinn threw herself down on the old lounge, and in five minutes was snoring as usual. Dil prepared Bess for bed, and rubbed her with a soft mitten she had made. The poor thing trembled so that it was a positive shudder. Then, as the snoring grew louder, they dared to give vent to their own overcharged hearts in tears.

"An' to think poor Christiana's burnt up, an' we can't tell how she got out of the giant's hands! Dil, there's jes' such truly people, an' mammy's one of 'em! Jes' think if she'd been like Christiana, an' took us by the hand, an' was leadin' us to heaven, an' pushin' the kerrige whiles to spell you!"

Then they cried again at the thought, so utterly delightful, and the present reality so hard to bear.

"But we know she *did* get to heaven," resumed Bess; "only we can't tell how many things there were. Dil, it isn't reel easy to go to heaven, after all. But when we have *him*, you see he'll do the fightin', an' he'll pick out the way, an' we'll go right straight along. We won't stop in them queer places an' get all tangled up; for we're in such a norful hurry to get there, an' have my hurted legs made well."

Dil kissed her convulsively, and cried over the shining golden head. Besides the book, there had been an irreparable loss to her, that Bess had not yet realized. She had tucked her precious picture inside the cover of the book. For now she felt it must be kept out of her mother's sight, as she could not explain how she came by it, and escape with her life. That, too, had perished in the flames, the next precious thing to Bess.

The poor children unlocked arms presently, and Dil crept into bed sad and forlorn. She heard Owen stealing in, but her mother never stirred.

Mrs. Quinn sat taking her cup of coffee the next morning when Owen made his appearance. She tried to recall what had happened last night, and whether she had thrashed him or not.

"A purty time of night it was for ye to come home," she began.

"Oh, come off!" said Owen. "What yer givin' us? I was home an' abed afore ye kem in, an' ye was full of the shindy at Mis' MacBride's. Don't ye remimber how ye wint on?"

Owen dodged the cuff. His mother was so nonplussed that for once she was helplessly silent. But as she went out of the door she turned and said,—

"I'll see yer in to-night, young feller."

Dil's face was in such a maze of surprise that she looked at Owen without being able to utter a word for some moments, while he laughed heartily.

"How could ye, Owny?"

"How cud I?" Owen laughed again. "Well," with a swagger, "it's all in knowin' how to dale with the female sect. Was she thunderin' mad last night? Did she go fer me?"

"But about Mrs. MacBride? How could ye know what happened?"

"Why, ye see I was passin' jes' after the shindy. That Mrs. Whalen who made the row whin she beat ye so, ye know, was harang'in'; an' then I heard there'd been a great row, an' mammy'd come home mad as a hornet. So, sez I, I'll wait until she's asleep before I trust myself. An' its jes' havin' yer wits about ye. She was too drunk to remember what she did. Did she break yer head agen? If she did I'll go an' complain of her. Whin yer tired a-havin' her round, we'll git her sent up to th' Island. An' now get me some grub."

"She only struck me wunst. But she burnt up something," and Dil began to sob. "But, Owny, ye were not in, an' it was a—a—"

"Git off de stump wid yer high notions! I'd save me head wid any kind o' lie. You gals don't know nothin' but to run right agin de stun wall. Ye see, it's a bit o' circumvention, an' ye jes' use yer brains a bit to save yer skull er yer back. But dat old gin-mill ain't goin' to boss me much longer. Ye'll see, an' be moighty s'prised. An' here's a nickel, Dil."

Owen ate his breakfast, and then taking out a cigarette, lighted it, and swaggered off.

Dil woke Dan, and gave him his meal, as two babies were asleep and the other sat on the floor munching a crust.

Bess slept late. Poor Dil went about her work in a strange maze. Owny slipped out of a great many things, and told lies about them, and this morning he had been very "cute." Dil sighed. She could not have done it. She would have blundered and betrayed herself. And yet she had told a lie about the book. It had not saved the book, but perhaps it had saved her and Bess from something more terrible.

It was a sad day for both of them. The babies were cross. One had a bad cold and a croupy sound in his voice. There was not even a glint of sunshine at noon now; the high houses kept it out of the court. But the day wore to an end. Mrs. Quinn did not go out at all in the evening. Owen was very jaunty, and pretended to study.

Mrs. Quinn's reformation lasted two or three days. She had "taken her oath she would niver step fut inside o' Mrs. MacBride's dure;" but Mrs. MacBride had no notion of losing so good a customer. To be sure, Mrs. Quinn was getting rather quarrelsome and overbearing, but she was good company for the most part.

Winter had fairly set in with December. There was much talk of dull times, and the babies fell off after Monday and Tuesday. Owen and his mother seemed continually on the warpath. He was a big, stout boy of his age; and, when he thought it was safe, played hookey, put in coal, ran errands, sold papers, and did whatever his hands found to do with all his might, even to snivyin' on the corner grocer. Dan was pretty shrewd and sharp, though not so daring, but could swear and smoke cigar ends with the worst of them.

There was an occasional religious visitor in the court besides the sisters and the priests. But Dil never mentioned them to her mother now. Besides, she did not want to leave Bess for even an hour or two at the Mission School; she hated to spend a moment away from her. Since the loss of the book and the picture they clung closer to each other. There was only one anticipation now, waiting for spring and John Travis.

And as other things failed, their faith seemed to centre about this. They lived on the hope of heaven with the fervor of saints who had known and loved the Lord, and were counting all the appointed days, as if the glories had already been revealed, and they were walking by faith.

VIII—BESS

Everybody began to talk about Christmas. Last year Dil had wheeled Bess around to see the shop windows.

"If it would come reel nice and warm, an' there wasn't any babies! But it's awful cold when you just have a winder open to sweep, an' I couldn't stan' bein' out in it."

"No, you couldn't," and Dil sighed.

Bess was ethereal now. Her large, bright eyes, her golden hair, and the pink that came in her cheeks every afternoon, gave a suggestion of the picture. Then she was so curiously, so nervously alive, that, afraid as Dil was of every change, she blindly hoped some of these things were indications of recovery.

But Dil's poor head ached a good deal now, and she had restless nights when it seemed as if she would burn up. As she listened to Bess's beautiful thoughts and strange visions, she felt discouraged with her own stupidness. She was so physically worn out that her brain was inert.

"I wisht I knew what Christmas was all about," sighed Bess. "An' Santa Claus! Mammy says there ain't no such thing, an' he couldn't come down a chimbly. But he gives a norful lot of things to some folks. An', Dil, we used to hang up our stockings. What's it for, anyway?"

Dil gave a long sigh, and the wrinkles of perplexity deepened and strayed over her short nose.

"Johnny Dike's goin' to see the cradle in the manger on Christmas Eve. An' he's goin' to take a present, some money he's been savin' up. What makes Christ get born agen? 'Tain't the Lord Jesus, though; for he's a big man now, if he can carry children in his arms."

"We might ast Johnny or Misses Murphy," suggested Dil.

"They're Catholics. An' there's such curis things, with people tellin' you diff'rent. I don't see how he can be born every Christmas. I b'lieve I like Santa Claus best. You don't have to give him nothin' when you ain't got even a penny. O Dil," pausing to rest a moment, "don't you wisht *he* was here! He'd know all about it. Rich folks have chances, an' get to know everything. He's a long way off. When mammy was clever t'other night, I ast her 'bout comin' crost the oshin, 'Lantic Oshin, 'tis; an' she said you sailed an' sailed two whole weeks. An' if he don't start 'till April, there'll be two weeks more. I keep countin' thim up."

Dil had been warming some broth.

"I wisht you'd take a little of this," she said. "The 'Spensary doctor said you must have it. An' you ain't eat nothin' but the pear an' the piece of norange."

"They was so good and juicy. My throat's hot, an' kinder dry an' sore. Things don't taste good."

"I wisht I could get some more of that nice medicine. The 'Spensary stuff ain't no good. I might ast Patsey to lend me some money; but how'd I ever get any to pay him back?"

They looked at each other in wonderment. Then the child's feverish eyes sparkled.

"O Dil, I know *he'd* help us pay it back, for mammy was so cross to the lady he sent that she won't come no more. An' 'twouldn't been no use to give mammy the money. O Dil, we've had ten whole dollars. Wasn't it lovely? An' I wisht the time would spin round an' round, faster'n ever. I get so tired waitin'. Seems sometimes 's if I jes' couldn't draw another breath."

"Oh, you must! you must!" cried Dil in affright. "For when people stop breathin', they die."

"An' I wanter live, so's we can get started for heaven. I'll be better when it's all nice an' warm out o' doors, an' sunshiny. I'd jes' like to live in sunshine. You see, when the babies cry, it makes me feel all roughened up like. An' I'm that feared o' mammy when she an' Owny hev scrimmiges. There's a lump comes in my throat 'n' chokes me. But I'm gonter live. Don't you know how las' winter I was so poor an' measlin'? An' I crawled out in the spring. Owny was readin' in his lesson 'bout some things doin' that way;" and Bess gave a pitiful ghost of a laugh.

"Won't you lay me down?" she asked presently. "My poor back's so tired."

"You must eat some broth first."

She did not want it, and the effort she made to please Dil was heroic.

She often asked to be laid down now. When the babies cried, it seemed as if knives were being thrust into her head. She had so many queer fancies, but she tried not to tell the bad ones to Dil. One moment she seemed out of doors, with the cold rasping her skin everywhere, going down her back like a stream of ice-water. Then she was scorched with heat, her skin crisping up and cracking. When she was pillowed up, it seemed as if she would fall to pieces; when she was laid down, the poor bones ached.

And in that land of "pure delight" there was no pain, no sickness, no chilling winds! And perhaps the babies didn't cry,—maybe there were no babies.

They mightn't be big enough to go, and they would be scared at the giants.

Monday night began badly. A neighbor came in and made a complaint about Owen, and threatened to have him arrested. He had broken a pane of glass and kicked her dog. Mrs. Quinn was tired with a big wash; and this made her furious, though she went at the woman in no gentle terms.

Owen had not been so much to blame. The miserable little cur had snapped at him, and he had kicked it away. Then, as it ran yelping along, it was too good a mark for a boy to miss. He shied a piece of oyster shell; but, as bad luck would have it, he missed the dog, and the missile bounded down to a basement window.

"I'll put that lad in the 'form school this blissid week! A pore woman can't take care o' sich a lot o' brats, an' they fuller 'n an egg of diviltry. I'll jist see —"

She began to hunt around for the end of a stout trunk-strap. Dil trembled in every limb. If Owny would only stay away! But he didn't. He came up the stairs whistling gayly; for he had earned a quarter, and he was saving money to have a regular Christmas blow-out.

His mother fell on him. There was a tremendous battle. Owen kicked and scratched and swore, and his mother's language was not over choice. He managed to wriggle away, and reached the door, crying out, as he sprang down the stairs, that he'd "niver darken the dure agin, if he lived a hundred years;" and added to it an imprecation that made Dil turn faint and cold.

Bess went into a hysteric.

"Drat the young un! Shet yer head, er you'll get some, ye bag o' bones! Ye shud a ben in yer grave long ago. Take her in t'other room, Dil. I can't bide the sight uv her!"

Dil uttered not a word, though the room spun round. She poured her mother a cup of tea, and had a dish of nicely browned sausage, and some baked potatoes. Mrs. Quinn ate, and threatened dire things about Owny. Then she put on her shawl, throwing it over her head, which meant an hour or two or three at Mrs. MacBride's, though she started to look for Owen.

Dil brought the wagon back, and nursed and soothed Bess.

"I wouldn't ever come back, if I was Owny," she said in her spasmodic tone, for the nervous fright was still strong upon her. "An' if I had two good legs, we'd run away too. Dil, I think she'd jes' be glad to have me die."

Dilsey Quinn shuddered. Just a few months longer—

Mrs. Murphy came in to borrow a "bit o' tay," and to learn what the rumpus was about. Dan told the story, putting Owny in the best light, and declaring valiantly that "Owny wasn't no chump."

"Misses Murphy," said Dil, as soon as she could get a chance, "what is it 'bout Christmas? an' what makes Christ be born ivery year?"

"Shure, dear, I do be havin' so many worries that I disremember. What wid th' babby bein' sick, an' pore ol' Mis' Bolan not sittin' up a minnit, an' bein' queer like in her mind, an' me hardly airnin' enough to keep body an' sowl togither, I hardly mind 'bout the blissed day. But I do be thinkin' he isn't born reely, for ye see the blissid Virgin's his mother, an' she's in hivin wid th' saints. I do be a bad hand at tellin' things straight; but I niver had any larnin', fer I wint in a mill whin I was turned o' six years. An' whin ye can't rade, it's hard gettin' to know much. But I'll ast the praist. Ah, dear," with a furtive glance at Dil, "If ye'd only let me ast him to come—"

"Oh, no, no!" protested Dil. "Mother'd kill us; an' she don't b'leve in priests an' such. You know how she went on 'bout the man who came an' sang."

"Ah, yis, dear; it wouldn't do." And she shook her head, her eyes still fixed sorrowfully on Bess. "But I have me beads, an' I go to confission wanst a month, an' that'll be Friday now, an' I'll ast Father Maginn an' tell ye all. Oh, you poor childer! An' it'll be a sad Christmas fer many a wan, I'm thinkin'. There's poor Mis' Bolan—"

Mrs. Murphy paused. Was Dil so blind? She could not suggest Mrs. Bolan's death when the great shadow seemed so near them.

"Dear," she added, with sympathetic softness, "if ye should be wantin' any one suddint like, run up fer me."

"Yer very kind, Misses Murphy. I sometimes wisht there would be nights a whole week long, I'm so tired."

Owen did not come home that night nor the next. Dil devoutly hoped he would not come at all. She had a secret feeling that he would go to Patsey, and she comforted Bess with it. The house was so much quieter, and Dan was better alone.

Even in Barker's Court there were people who believed in Christmas, though some of them had ideas quite as vague as Dilsey Quinn's. But there was a stir in the very air, and penny trumpets began to abound. Still, there were many who had no time for Christmas anticipations, who were driven to do their six days' work in five, who stitched from morning to midnight, who did not even have time to gossip with a neighbor.

Poor Bess! she could not eat, and she was so restless. The pears and the oranges were gone, and, saddest of all, their bank was empty. If Patsey would only come!

Dil took Bess up and laid her down, gave her sips of water, caressed her tenderly, bathed her head with cologne, and even that was running low. The babies were left on the floor to cry, if Dil caught the faintest sound that was like desire. Bess often just held up her spindling arms and, drawing Dil down, kissed her with eager fervor.

She was so glad to have night come and see the last baby taken away. Mrs. Quinn was working at a grand house where they were to have a Christmas feast. She was to go again to-morrow; and, as it was late, she did not go out, but just tumbled into bed, with not an anxiety on her mind.

Dil sat and crooned to her little sister, who seemed a part of her very life. When Mrs. Quinn snored, it was safe to indulge in a little freedom. And though Dil was so worn and weary, she ministered as only love can. Everybody had been so used to Bess's weakness, and they thought that the end would be a great relief. But Dil never dreamed of the end they saw so plainly.

It was past midnight when Dil laid her down for the last time.

"O Dil, I feel so nice an' easy all of a suddent," she cried, with an eager joyousness that thrilled the heavy heart. "Nothin' pains me. I'm quite sure I'll be better to-morrow. An' when Patsey comes, we'll just ast him to help us get that nice medicine. He's so good to us, Dil; 'n' if he had lots of money he'd give us anything."

"He just would," said Dil. "An' if Owny's gone to him, he'll be all right."

The thought comforted her immeasurably.

"O Dil, dear," murmured the plaintive voice, "do you remember the big bowl of wild roses, an' how sweet they were, an' how pritty, with their soft pink leaves an' baby buds? I can almost smell them. It's so sweet all around. Dil, *are* there any wild roses?"

"No, dear," said the gentle, tired voice.

"Well—then I'm dreamin'; an' they're so lovely. Just like *he* told us, you know; 'bout that place where they growed. Oh, you dear, sweet, lovely Dil! I want to see the picture he put you in. You were pritty, I know; folks always are pritty in pictures. An' we'll ast him to let us be taken over agen, for when we get on the way to heaven we'll both be so full of joy. An' he'll help us clear to the pallis."

She stopped to breathe. It came so quick and short now, hardly going below her chest.

"Sit here an' hold my two hands. Dil, dear, I'm as much trouble as the babies; but I most know I'll be better to-morrow. And when I go fast asleep, you run right to bed, an' it'll be all right. I feel so light an' lovely, 'most 's if I was a wild rose—a soft, pink, satiny wild rose."

There was a little pleasant gurgle that did duty for a laugh. Dil kissed her and crooned sleepily. As she held the hands, the fever seemed to go out of them. The little golden head had such a restful poise. The breath came slowly, easily.

Dil kissed her with the long, yearning, passionate kisses that take one's whole soul, that leave some souls bankrupt indeed. All her own being was in a strange quiver. Oh, did it mean that Bess would be better to-morrow? She believed it in some strange, undefined way, and was at peace.

Perhaps she drowsed. She started, feeling stiff and chilly. Bess slept tranquilly. There was no pain to make her moan unconsciously. Why, it was almost a foretaste of that blessed land.

Dil wrapped herself in an old shawl and dropped down on her little cot. In all the glad wide world there was no one to come in and comfort her, and so God sent his angel—kindly sleep. The night breath that he breathed over her had the fragrance of wild roses.

The alarm clock roused her. It was dark now when her day began. Bess was quiet; and she drew the blanket more closely around her, for the morning felt bitterly cold. She stirred the fire, made her mother's coffee, and broiled a bit of steak. The windows were all ice, which seldom happened.

"It's enough to kill one to go out in the cold," declared Mrs. Quinn. "I'll not be home airly the night, for I promised cook to stay a bit an' gev her a hand wid th' fancy fixin's. Foine doin's they're to be havin'. An' if that thafe of the world Owny comes in, ye be soft spoken jist as if nothin' had happened. I'll settle wid him. I'll gev him some Christmas!"

With that she was off. Then Dan came for his breakfast.

"I do miss Owny so," he half whimpered. "Ther' ain't a boy in the street who could think up such roarin' fun."

"Whisht!" Dil said softly. "Bess is asleep, an' I won't have her worrited. She had a bad time yist'day with the babies. I do hope there won't be no such crowd to-day. Seven babies an' that was thirty-five cents. Mother might be given Bess an' me some Christmas."

Dan laughed at that.

Dil sighed. She drank a little coffee, but she could not eat. Two sleepy babies came. She washed the dishes, and spread up her mother's bed, putting the babies in there. It was dark, with no ventilation but the door, and kept warm easily.

Another and another baby, one crying for its mother. When Dil had hushed it she took a vague glance at Bess, whose fair head lay there so restful. The frost was melting off the window-panes, and she put out the lamp. With a baby in her arms she sat down and rocked.

A curious sense of something, not quite anxiety, came over her presently. She went to Bess and raised the blanket, peering at the small white face that seemed almost to light the obscurity of the room. The eyes were half-closed. The lips were parted with a smile, and the little white teeth just showed. One hand seemed to hold up the chin.

Dil stooped and kissed her. O God! what was it? What was it? For Bess was marble cold.

"O Bess, Bess!" she cried in mortal terror. "Wake up, my darlin'! Wake up an' get warm."

As she seized the hand, a startling change came over the child. The chin dropped. The pretty smile was gone. The eyes looked out with awesome fixedness. Her heart stood still as if she were frozen.

Then, moved by horror, she flew up-stairs, her breath almost strangling her.

"O Misses Murphy!" she shrieked, "there's somethin' strange come over Bess. She's never been like this—an' cold—"

"Yis, dear. I'll jist look at poor Mis' Bolan. She do be goin' very fast. All night she was that res'les' talkin' of the beautiful hymn the man sung, an' beggin' him to sing it agen; an' then hearin' angels an' talkin' 'bout green fields an' flowers, an' where there do be no night. They do be mostly so at the last, rememberin' beautiful things."

An awful terror clutched Dil at the heart, as she recalled Bess's talk of the wild roses. So cruel a fear smote her that her very tongue seemed paralyzed.

"You don't mean"—she cried wildly.

Mrs. Murphy's thoughts were running on Mrs. Bolan.

"She'll not last the day through. Pore dear, there's not much pleasure to the'r ould lives. But she did be so longin' to have that man come agen—"

She had taken Dil's hand, and they were going down-stairs. A baby had rolled off the lounge and bumped his head, and was screaming. But Dil hardly heard him. They went through to the tiny room.

"Ah, pore dear! Pore lamb! She's gone, an' she's outen all her mis'ry. She'll niver suffer any more. An' she's safe—"

Mrs. Murphy paused, not quite sure she could give that comfort. There was purgatory, and the poor thing had never been christened. She was extremely ignorant of her own church doctrine; but she felt the bitter injustice of condemning this poor soul to everlasting torment for her mother's neglect.

"No, Misses Murphy," cried Dil in the accent of utter disbelief, "she can't be —Oh, hurry an' do somethin' for her. She's jes fainted! Le's get her warm agen. Bring her out to the fire, an' I'll run for the 'Spensary doctor. Oh, no, she isn't—she wouldn't—'cause we was goin' to heaven together in the spring, an' she couldn't leave me without a word—don't you see?"

Oh, the wild, imploring eyes that pierced Mrs. Murphy through! the heart-breaking eyes that entreated vainly, refusing the one unalterable fiat!

"Ah, dear, they'sen don't hev any ch'ice. O Dil, Dilly Quinn!" and she clasped the child to her heart. "You mustn't take on so, dear! Shure, God knows best. Mebbe he's better'n folks an' the things they say. She won't suffer any more, pore dear. I've seen it for weeks, an' knowed what must come."

Dil gave a few long, dry, terrible sobs; then she lay helpless in Mrs. Murphy's arms. The kind soul placed her on the cot, sprinkled water on her face, chafed her hands; but Dil lay as one dead.

Then she ran down-stairs.

"O Mrs. Minch! have ye iver a bit of camphire? I used the last o' mine this mornin' for the pore old craythur. Bessy Quinn's gone at last, an' is cold, an' Dil's that overcome she's gone in an norful faint. Come up a bit, do. An' that haythen woman'll not care more'n if it was a kitten. She do be the hardest!"

Mrs. Minch laid down her work, looked up the "camphire," and plied her caller with inquiries.

All their efforts were unavailing, though Dil opened her eyes once, and at intervals a shudder ran through her frame.

"Yes, the poor dear's dead and cold, and it's God's mercy, Mrs. Murphy. How she's lived so long's a mystery; but Dil's been more watchful than most any mother. She was the sweetest and patientest, and loved her beyond all things. Mrs. Quinn hasn't any human feeling in her, and there's plenty like her, more's the shame. When you bring helpless little ones in the world, it's not their fault. And when they are bruised and banged and made helpless, as that poor little one, a mother's heart should have pitied her."

"Oh, dear, it's the rum that takes out all the nateral feelin'. An' one 'ud think she'd had enough of it in her husband, not to be goin' the same way. An' pore Dil carin' for them babies an' doin' a woman's work, a-stuntin' her an' makin' her old afore her time. An', if ye'll stay, I'll go fer th' 'Spensary doctor. Sorra a Christmas it'll be in the court. Mr. Sheehan is dyin', an' Mrs. Neefus's baby went yes'tday, an' the ould woman—but they do be dyin' all the time, some wan."

Mrs. Minch bent over Dil with pitying eyes. She had seen better times, and lived in a nicer neighborhood than Barker's Court. But poverty had driven her down step by step. She had her old deaf father to care for, and a son growing up; and the three rooms, such as they were, proved cheaper than anything she had seen, though she was on the lookout all the time. She had not made much intimacy with her neighbors, except that through her pity for Mrs. Bolan she had come to know good-hearted Mrs. Murphy quite well, and she had been interested in Dilsey and Bess. But most of the people in the court were afraid of Mrs. Quinn's tongue.

"The poor thing!" she sighed. "She is a little old woman already. She has never had leave to grow as children should. Oh, why are they brought into the world to suffer?"

She had once thought herself full of trust and love to God, but so many questions had come to the surface with her years of hard experience. Why this little Bess should have suffered four years—but both parents had given her a good constitution, that in some positions in life might have made her a useful factor instead of mere waste material.

Then she took up one of the crying babies. Another was clamoring loudly, "Bed, bed," and opening wide his mouth to show her how empty it was.

"Oh, how ever did she look after them all?" she cried in despair as Mrs. Murphy entered.

"She had a rare way with childers, that she had." Mrs. Murphy cut a chunk from the loaf of bread and gave the hungry baby. "An' the docthor will be in as soon as he kin, but there's a sight o' folks waitin'. I have heerd say a grane Christmas made fat graveyards, but this is cold enough to be black. An' how's the poor gurl?"

"She seems—asleep somehow, and you can notice her breathin'."

"I'll look after Mrs. Bolan, an' kem down agen," said Mrs. Murphy, disappearing.

IX—DILSEY

Mrs. Bolan was faintly breathing, as she had been since midnight, but so cold that she might easily be thought dead. Mrs. Murphy's baby was asleep.

The babies were crowing and talking in their fashion, unmindful of sorrow.

"The pore dear," said Mrs. Murphy tenderly, viewing Bess; "I'm thinkin' we better care for her afore Dil wakes up. An' she never havin' had a bit o' christenin', along o' Mrs. Quinn not belevin' nothin'. I've heard her talk a way that wud set yer blood a-chill."

"The Lord took the little ones in his arms and said, 'Forbid them not,' and I guess he won't mind the christenin'. And this child's been patient and cheerful beyond common. I think she's had a lot of Christian grace unbeknownst. She'd look up with her sweet smile that almost broke your heart, when Dil would be takin' her out. And how she stood everything—"

"Mrs. Quinn's been not so savage as she used. 'Tain't nat'rel for mothers to be so cruel. But 'twas last March, if I don't disremember—you were not here then, Mrs. Minch—she made such a nawful 'ruction that the neighbors called in de cop, and nothin' but her beggin' off an' sayin' the children wud starve, an' promisin' on her bended knees, which she never uses fer a bit o' prayer, saved her. An' she don't bang 'em about quite so bad since."

"There was an awful time the other night."

"Yes; that Owny's too smart, an' mebbe he would er banged her in a fair fight; but he cut stick, an' hasn't shown hide ner hair sence."

Mrs. Murphy leaned over Dil, and uttered a benison in her ignorant Christianity.

"'Pears like they jist oughten to go togither. She looks like a ghost, poor thing." Then she lifted Bess from the shabby wagon that had been her home so long, and brought her out on the lounge.

"Will ye look at them poor legs?" she said with a cry. "They do make yer heart bleed. She was a smart little thing, goin' to school, whin it happened. The father oughter been hung fer it; fer it was he that did it, murderin' by inches. An' he beat Mrs. Quinn to a jelly. Wudden't ye think now she'd had enough o' rum, not to be goin' the same road?"

Mrs. Minch sighed.

"It's stuck everywhere, right in a body's way, Mrs. Murphy. They're taxin' people for prisons and 'sylums and homes for orphans, when they haven't the sense to shut up the saloons and gin-mills. Look at that Mrs. MacBride, smilin' and making it pleasant for a hard-workin' woman, havin' a nice warm room for gossipin' and such, and bein' clever enough to make them run up a score, and get her money once a week. There's no dancin' nor carousin'; but it takes in the decentish sort of women, and turns 'em out as bad as the men. It's the poor families that's pinched and starved and set crazy. When I think of my boy growin' up in it—but where'll poor folks go? Saloons are all over. They fight for the chance to ruin folks."

"Thrue for ye, Mrs. Minch. An' sorra indade it is whin ye do be sad that they come into the world, an' rej'ice whin they go out of it young. They're spared a dale o' pain an' care. Yet it do seem wrong some way. Childers should be a blessin' an' comfort to yer ould age. Things is changed in the world. One gits that confused with thinkin'—"

They had prepared some water, but the poor little body was clean and sweet. It was heart-breaking to see it.

Mrs. Murphy went into the bedroom for some clothing.

"Will ye look at the sort o' bury Dil made out o' boxes an' covered. She's that handy an' full o' wit. An' them clo'es is like snow, and all mended nate. I don't see how she cud do it wid all the babies. An' I do be thinkin' it was Dil's love that kep' the little wan alive so long. It was like medicine; her warm arms an' cheery smile, her patience an' thinkin' what wud pleasure Bess. If there don't be a straight road to hiven fer thim both—an' purgatory ought to be saved fer the ither kind. Now, it don't look a bit sinsible that little lamb shud suffer whin she's suffered so much a'ready! Sometimes I most think the church has mistook whin they save the rumsellers an' the great wicked men wid their money, cause they kin pay fer prayers."

"She's in heaven, if there is any heaven." Sometimes Mrs. Minch doubted.

"An' oh, Mrs. Minch, if there wasn't any hiven to rest us at last, how cud we live through the cruel world?"

Such a pathetic cry as it was!

The doctor came. He looked at Bess, and asked a few questions, made a note or two in his book, cutting short Mrs. Murphy's explanations.

"Yes, yes; I've seen the child. She's been strung on fine steel wires, or they'd given way long ago. And the old woman? Strange how they go on living when they had a hundred times better be dead, and the people of some account go out like the snuff of a candle! Where's the girl?" glancing around.

"In there." Mrs. Murphy nodded towards the room.

Dil lay motionless, but for the faint breathing. The doctor listened with his ear down on her heart, felt her pulse, and seemed in a study.

"Let her sleep as long as she can. She has worn herself out. She used to wheel this one round," nodding. "Have in some fresh air; the room is stifling. How any one lives—"

Dil roused without opening her eyes.

"Was it you, Bess? Oh, *is* it morning?"

"No, no; go to sleep again. The night's just begun. She's dead tired out," to the women. "Let the mother come round when she can, and get rid of these young ones before the girl wakes. If there's anything else wanted, send round. Are these people very poor?"

"Mrs. Quinn goes out washing. And the babies are taken in by the day. I don't know"—doubtfully.

"The mother will settle that. And the old lady—the city must bury her, I suppose?"

"'Deed an' it must. She's had nothin' but her pinshin, an' has no folk."

They found Bess's nice white frock pinned up in a cloth, beautifully ironed and laid away in anticipation of the journey—the very journey she had taken so unknowingly. They put it on, and smoothed down the poor little legs with tender hands. Then they laid her on her mother's bed until Dil should rouse.

Mrs. Minch brought up her sewing, while Mrs. Murphy went to her own room to look after Mrs. Bolan. Mrs. Carr, another neighbor, came in and helped with the babies, and wondered how Dilly Quinn had ever been able to do as much work as a hearty, grown woman, and she not bigger than a ten-year-old child!

It was three o'clock when Dil roused. Mrs. Minch sat quietly at her sewing. The wagon was pushed clear up to the window, empty.

"O Mrs. Minch, what has happened?" She sprang out, wild-eyed and quivering.

"My dear," Mrs. Minch took her in her arms, "Bess is better off. She is in heaven with the good God, who will be tenderer of her than any human friend. She will have no more pain. She will be well and strong, and a lovely angel. You would not wish her back—"

"Yes, I do, I do. We was goin' to heaven together in the spring; we had it all planned. And Bess wouldn't 'a' gone without me—oh, I know she wouldn't.

Where is she? What have you done with her?"

"She is in there."

Dil flew to her mother's room. The ironing-board lay on the bed, and a strange, still shape imperfectly outlined under the sheet.

"She looks like an angel," said Mrs. Minch.

Dilsey Quinn stared, bereft of her senses for some moments. Slowly the incidents of the morning came over her—of last night, when Bess seemed so improved, so hopeful. She had seen dead people. Death was no stranger in Barker's Court. There were "wakes," and quiet, hurried burials. They died and were taken away, that was all. With a curious, obstinate unreason she knew Bess had died like all the rest; yet she had been so sure Bess could not die. But she had *not* gone to heaven. The breath had gone out of her body, but a breath couldn't go to heaven. She had left her body here; the poor hurted legs the Lord Jesus would have mended. They could never be mended now, for they would be put in the ground.

She stood so still that Mrs. Minch raised the sheet. The pinched look was going out of the face, as it often does after death. The eyes were closed; the long bronze lashes were beautiful; the thin lips had been pressed rather tightly, as if in fear that they might betray their secret. Yet it had a strange, serene beauty.

Dil did not cry or utter a sound. A great solitude enveloped her, as if she were alone in a wide desert. She would never have any one to love or caress; a thick darkness settled all about her, as if now she and Bess were shut out of heaven forever. For what would the palace be, and the angels innumerable, if Bess was not there?

She turned and went to her own room, began to pick up the things and tidy it, spread the cot, shook the cushion of the poor dilapidated wagon, carefully laid over it the blanket she had taken so much pains to make.

"Mrs. Minch," she said, "will you please bring Bess in here. Mammy wouldn't like her there. An' I want her here—on my bed."

Mrs. Minch looked at her in surprise. The face was rigid and unresponsive, but there was an awesome, chilling sorrow in every line. She reverently obeyed Dil's behest.

"You are very good. You see, no one cared 'bout her but jes' me an' Patsey an'"—Ah, what *would* John Travis say? "An' I want to keep her here."

"My dear, dear child—"

She put away the kindly hands, not ungently, but as if she could not quite bear

84

them—as if she was too sore for any human touch.

"How did I come to sleep so long?" she asked, in a strained, weary tone.

"You were so tired, poor dear. The doctor was in, and he said it was the best thing for you. Mrs. Murphy has been in and out, and Mrs. Carr."

"You took care of the babies?" Her lips quivered, and a few big tears rolled down her cheeks. She could suffer, if the time to sorrow had not yet come.

"Yes, dear. I don't see how you get along so with them. And do you feel better?"

The kind eyes studied her with concern.

"I'm well. I never do get sick."

"Do you know where your mother is?"

"Not the street. No, ma'am. The people have a queer long name. An' she'll be late th' night."

Mrs. Murphy looked in the door.

"Ah, yer up, an' ye do look better. Hev ye had anything to ate? Do ye mind if I have Mrs. Minch come up-stairs just a bit?"

"Oh, no." Dil did not notice the strain in the eyes, the awesomeness of facing death.

"I cudden't be alone. She's roused, but she's almost gone; fightin' fer life, one may say, at the very end," she whispered as they went up the stairs.

The babies were amusing themselves. Dil uncovered the face of her dead, and looked long and earnestly, as if she knew there was a great mystery she ought to solve. Ah, how sweet she was! Dil's heart swelled with a sense of triumph. She had always been so proud of Bess's beauty.

But what was *dead*? It happened any time, and to anybody, to babies mostly, and made you cold and still, useless. Then you were taken away and buried. It was altogether different from going to heaven. What strange power had taken Bess, and kept her from that blessed journey? Why did the Lord Jesus let any one do it? John Travis couldn't have been so mistaken, and Christiana, and the children.

She was so glad they had put on her best dress, bought with John Travis's money. Ah, if they only had started that day and risked all! Here was her blue sash and the blue bows for her sleeves. She hardly had the courage to touch the beloved form.

How strangely cold the little hands were. She kissed them, and then she no longer felt afraid. She raised the frail figure, and passed the ribbon round the waist. Almost it seemed as if Bess breathed.

She brought the brush and comb, and curled the hair in her own flowing fashion, picking out the pretty bang in rings, kissing the cold cheeks, the shell-like eyelids. Why, surely Bess was only asleep. She must, she would waken, to-morrow morning perhaps. A sudden buoyant hope electrified her. She had her again, and the horrible thought of separation vanished. Dil was too ignorant to formulate any theories, but every pulse stirred within her own body.

Two of the mothers came for babies, but she uttered no word of what had happened. Then she fed the others, and fixed the fire, and Dan peered in fearfully. She gave him a slice of bread, and he was glad to be off.

Up-stairs they had watched the breath go out of the poor body.

"Pore thing! God rist her sowl wheriver it is," and Mrs. Murphy crossed herself.

"Has she no friends?"

"Not a wan, I belayve. She used to talk of some nevys whin she first come, that's nigh two years ago. But she'd lost track of them. I'm sure I've taken good care of the pore ould craythur, an' I hope some wan will do the same to me at the last."

"You're a kindly woman, Mrs. Murphy, and God grant it. We don't know where nor when the end will come."

Mrs. Minch stopped as she went down-stairs.

"Poor old Mrs. Bolan has gone to the better land. She and Bess will have a Christmas with the angels. They will not want to come back here."

Dil had no courage to argue. But she knew to the very farthest fibre of her being, that nothing could so change Bess that she would desire to stay anywhere without her.

Mrs. Garrick had heard the tidings before she came in for her baby, and was profuse in her sympathies.

"But it's the Lord's mercy, for she were a poor sufferer, and was jist waitin'. How did it happen? Was it in the night, whilst ye were all asleep? An' to think yer poor mother whint away knowin' nothin'."

"I can't talk about it. I—I don't know."

"An' old Mis' Bolan. Well, I'll run up-stairs a bit, an' see Mrs. Murphy."

She was rewarded for her trouble here; the strange curiosity of some, as if the dead face could answer the mystery.

"She's a moighty quare girl, that Dilsey Quinn. Niver to be askin' one to look at the corpse; an' if Bess hadn't been so peaked, she would have been a pritty child. She had such iligant hair."

The neighbors began to make calls of condolence. Two deaths in a house was an event rather out of the common order of things.

Dil awed them by her quiet demeanor, and answered apathetically, busying herself with the supper.

"What hev ye done wid her?" asked one. "Shure, she's not bin tuk away?"

"No; she's in ther', in my room. An'—an' she's mine."

For to Dil there seemed something sacred about Bess, and she kept guard rigorously. It was not simply a dead body to gloat over. They could go up-stairs and look at Mrs. Bolan.

It was nine o'clock when her mother came home laden with budgets, and Dan following in a vaguely frightened manner. He had been hanging about Mrs. MacBride's, waiting for her. She had gone in and taken her "sup o' gin," and heard the news, also the complaints.

"Whiniver did it happen, Dil?" throwing down her budgets. "She's been no good to hersilf nor no wan else this long while. An' she cudden't iver git well, an' was a sight o' trouble. But I'm clear beat. Week after week I thought she'd be sure to go, but when you're lookin', the thing niver comes. An' it's took me so suddent like, that I had no breath left at all. Was it true—did ye find her dead, an' faint clear away?"

She looked rather admiringly at Dil.

"Yes—she were cold," said Dil briefly. "An' then I don't know what happened."

"Ye pore colleen! Ye'll be better widout her, an' ye'll be gittin well an' strong agin. It's bin a hard thing, an' yer divil of a father shud a had his own back broke. But he's fast enough, and I hope they'll kape him there. Any word of Owny?"

"No." Oh, what would Owny say—an' Patsey.

"Who kem an' streeked her? Let's see."

She took the lamp and went in. It seemed to Dil as if she would even now shake her fist at Bess, and the child stood with bated breath.

"She were a purty little thing, Dil," the mother said with a softened inflection. "Me sister Morna had yellow hair an' purplish eyes, and was that fair an' sweet, but timid like. I believe me mother had some such hair, but the rest of us had black. She looks raile purty, an' makes a better corpse than I iver thought. Why didn't ye lit thim see her, Dil? Ye's needn't a been shamed of her."

Dil was saved from answering by the advent of a throng of neighbors. The room seemed so warm, and there was such a flurry, she dropped on the lounge faint and breathless.

"Go to bed, Dan," said his mother.

Dil rose again and opened the door. The cold air, close and vile as it was, felt grateful.

"Go up-stairs a bit in Mrs. Murphy's;" and though the permission was a command, Dil went gratefully.

Mrs. Murphy sat sewing to make up for lost time. Her little girl was asleep in the cradle. She had improved since cooler weather had set in. The door of one room was shut. The old chintz-covered Boston rocker was empty.

"I couldn't stay to see them all lookin' at her," she exclaimed tremulously, as she almost tottered across the room.

"No, dear." Mrs. Murphy took her in her arms. "Ye look like a ghost. But Bess is main pritty, an' it's a custom. Will ye sit here?"

Dil shuddered as she looked at the empty chair where Mrs. Bolan used to sit.

"No; I'll take the stool. I just want to be a bit still like an' think. I couldn't talk 'bout *her*, you know."

"Yes, dear," with kindly sympathy.

Dil dropped on a box stool, leaning her folded arms on a chair. Mrs. Murphy took up her sewing again. She longed to comfort, but she was sore afraid the two lorn souls were wandering about purgatory. She had a little money of Mrs. Bolan's that she meant to spend in masses. But who would pay for a mass for Bessy Quinn's soul? And she had never been baptized. The ignorant, kindly woman was sore distressed.

Dil seemed to look through the floor and see the picture down-stairs. All her sense of possession rose in bitter revolt. Yet now she was helpless to establish her supreme right. Her mother had grudged Bess the frail, feeble spark of life; she alone had cared for her, loved her, protected her, and she was shut out, sent away. Now that Bess needed no care and lay there quiet, they could come and pity her.

Presently more tranquil thoughts came. Even her mother could not do anything to hurt Bess. She was safe at last.

There had been so much repression and self-control in Dil's short life, that it made her seem apathetic now. And yet, slowly as the poor pulses beat, there was a strange inward fire and stir, as if she must do something. A curious elusiveness shrouded the duty or work, and yet it kept hovering before her. Oh, what was it?

Did she fall asleep, and was it a vision, a vague remembrance of something she had heard? Bess was not dead, but in a strange, strange sleep. Once there had been a little girl in just this sleep, and One had come—yes, she would get up—about midnight these strange charms worked.

She would get up and go softly over to Bess. She would take the little hand in hers; she would kiss the pale, still lips, and say, "Bess, my darling, wake up. I can't live without you. You have had such a nice long rest. Open your eyes an' look at me. Bess, dear, you remember we are to go to heaven in the spring. *He* will be waitin' for us, an' wonderin' why we don't come. He is goin' to fight the giants, to show us the way, an' row us over the river to the pallis."

Then the eyes would open blue as the summer sky, the lips would smile, the little hands reach out and grow warm. There would be a strange quiver all through the body, and Bess would sit up and be alive once more. Oh, the glad cry of joy! Oh, the wordless, exquisite rapture of that moment! And Bess, in some mysterious way, would be better, stronger, and the days would fly by until the blessed spring came.

Mrs. Murphy touched her, and roused her from this trance of delight. She heard her mother's voice and started.

"It's a nice sleep ye've had," said Mrs. Murphy's kindly voice. "An' it's full bedtime, an' past. They've all gone, an' yer mother wants ye."

Dil groped her way down-stairs. There was a vicious smell of beer and kerosene-smoke in the warm room.

"It's time ye were in bed," said her mother. "Ye kin sleep in there," indicating her own room with a nod; "fer I'll not sleep the night with me child lyin' dead in the house. Bridget Malone has kem to stay wid me. We'll jist sit up."

"O mother," cried Dil, aghast, "let me sleep in my own room! I'd rather be there with Bess."

"Is the colleen's head turned wid grafe? Sleepin' wid a corpse! Who iver heerd of sich a thing? Indade ye'll not, miss! Go to bed at wunst, an' not a word outen you."

Her first impulse was to defy the woman looming up so tall and authoritative. But the shrewd sense that comes early to the children of poverty restrained her. She would be worsted in the end, so she went reluctantly. Had she dreamed? No, it must be true. She *could* waken Bess. Again the uplifting hope took possession of her. She seemed wafted away to a beautiful country with Bess. So absorbing was the vision that it filled her with a certainty beyond the faintest doubt. She did not even take off her dress, but lay there wide-eyed and rapturous.

After a while the chatter ceased and the snoring began. How still it was everywhere! But Dil was not afraid.

X—IN THE DESERT ALONE

Dilsey Quinn rose with a peculiar lightness of heart, and seemed walking on air. A curious tingle sped through her nerves, and her eyes had a strange light of their own. She pushed the door open and looked out cautiously. Her mother was on the lounge. Bridget sat by the stove, her chair tilted back against the door-jamb. The lamp had been turned down a little, the stove-lid lifted; and it made a strange, soft semicircle on the ceiling, such as Dil had seen around the heads in pictures when she had stolen a glance at the show windows.

The silence, for that impressed her, in spite of snoring in different keys, and the weird aspect, made the room instinct with supernatural life. Dil did not understand this, but she felt it, and was filled and possessed by that exaltation of mysterious faith. She walked softly but fearlessly across the room,—if she could open the door without Bridget hearing.

John Travis should have seen her at that moment, with the unearthly radiance on her face, the uplifted confident eyes.

Her small hand was on the knob. She opened the door—a moment more—

Alas! Bridget had an impression, and sprang up. Seeing the figure she uttered a wild shriek.

"A banshee! A banshee!" she cried in a spasm of terror.

Dil stood rooted to the spot. Mrs. Quinn sprang across the room.

"Hould yer murtherin' tongue!" she cried. "Why—it's Dil," seizing her by the shoulder. "Whativer are ye doin', walkin' in yer slape an' rousin' the house? An' yer' a fool, Bridget!"

Bridget Malone stared at the small grayish figure, unconvinced.

"Wake up, ye omadhoun!" and the mother shook Dil fiercely. "Ye can't do nothin' fer the child. Let her rist in peace; she's better off nor she's been this many a day."

"O Mrs. Quinn, don't be hard on the poor gurrul. She's bin dreamin' af the little wan, bein' so used to tindin' on her all hours af the night. But I thought sure it was Bess's ghost, bein' but half awake mesilf."

"Wid no legs to walk on!" was the sarcastic rejoinder.

"As af a ghost had need of legs! An' I won't be sittin' there by the dure—"

"Git back to yer bed, Dil, an' we won't have no more sich capers in the dead o' night, frightin' folks out of their sinsis."

She led Dil roughly back to her bed. Then for safe keeping she slipped the chair back just under the knob, and Dil was a prisoner in a black hole, a small improvement on that of Calcutta.

A whirlwind of passion swept over Dilsey Quinn—a pitiful, helpless passion. She could have screamed, she could have torn the bed-clothes to pieces, or stamped in that uncontrollable rage and disappointment. But she knew her mother would beat her, and she was too sore and helpless to be banged about.

Her mother would not let her bring Bess back to life if she knew. And she could not explain—there was nothing to be put in words. You just went and did it. Oh, it seemed as if something might have helped her, some great, strong power that made people rich and happy, and gave them so many lovely things. Bess was only such a little out of all the big world!

And now she would never, never come back. An awful, cold despair succeeded the passion. They could never go to heaven together. Bess was dead, just like Mrs. Bolan, like the people who died in the court. They would take her out and bury her. That was all!

An indescribable horror fell upon Dil. The horror of the solitude that comes of doubt and darkness, the ghost of that final solitude that seems watching at the gates of death. Bess had gone off, been swallowed up in it, and there was nothing, nothing!

The morning dawned at last. Dil, half-stifled with bad air, and racked with that fearful mental inquisition, collapsed. She seemed shrunken and old, as old as Mrs. Bolan. There was nothing more for her.

Bridget Malone was to stay. The two women had a cup of coffee together, then Mrs. Quinn went to see the 'Spensary doctor. When she came back they spread a sheet over the small table, and brought out the body of the dead child.

"Folks'll be comin' in to see it," she said with some pride. "An' she looks that swate no one need be ashamed of her! She'd been a purty girl but for the accidint, for that stopped her growin'. I've had a long siege wid her, the Lord knows! An' now I must run up to Studdemyer's an' tell 'em of the sorrow an' trouble, an' mebbe I'll get lave to do somethin' to-morrow. But I'll be back afore the men kim in."

Dil moved about silently, and went frequently into her own room. The intense fervor and belief of the night had vanished. The court children straggled in and stared, half-afraid. The women said she was better off and out of her trouble; and now and then one spoke of her being in heaven.

She was not in heaven, Dil knew. And how could she be better off in the cold, hateful ground than in her warm, loving arms?

One gets strangely accustomed to the dear dead face. Dil paid it brief visits when no one else was by. A little change had come over it,—the inevitable change; but to Dil it seemed as if Bess was growing sorry that she had died; that the little shrinking everywhere meant regret.

Mrs. Quinn came back with a gift from her sympathetic customer, who imagined she had found heroic motherly devotion in this poor woman who had four children to care for. There were numberless visitors who gossiped and were treated to beer—there was quite a dinner, with an immense steak to grace the feast.

Presently a man came in and took the measure of the body, and then went up-stairs. An hour later a wagon stopped before the court, and two men shouldered a coffin. The small one went into the Quinns'. It was of stained wood with a muslin lining, and the little body was laid in its narrow home. Then the attendant went up-stairs, and some of the women followed. There was a confusion of voices, then the two men came lumbering down the winding stairs with their load, slid it into the wagon, while a curious throng gathered round in spite of the chill blast. They came up again, one man with a screwdriver in his hand.

"Take a look at her, Dil. Poor dear, she's gone to her long rest."

Mrs. Quinn pushed her forward. The women fell back a little. The man put down the coffin lid,—it was all in one piece,—and began to screw it down.

Dil gave a wild shriek as it closed over the pretty golden head, and would have dropped to the floor, but some one caught her. The man completed his task, picked up the burthen, it was so light; and when Dil came out of her faint Bess, with two other dead bodies, was being jolted over the stones to a pauper's grave.

"Come now," began Mrs. Quinn, "it's full time ye wer sensible. She's dead, an' it's a blissid relase, an' she's got no more suf'frin' to go tru wid. It's bin a hard thrial, an' she not able to take a step this four year. Ye'd better go to bed an' rist, for ye look quare 'bout the eyes. Ye kin have my bed if ye like."

Dil shook her head, and tottered to her own little cot. "O Bess! Bess!" she cried in her heart, but her lips made no sound. How could people die who were not old nor sick? For *she* wanted to die, but she did not know how.

There were people around until after supper. Then two or three of them went down to Mrs. MacBride's. Mrs. Murphy promised to stay with Dil.

"Shure," said some one, "there'll be a third goin' out prisintly. It's bad luck when more than wan corpse goes over the trashold to wunst. An' that Dil don't look like long livin'. She's jist worn hersilf out wid that other poor thing."

In the evening Patsey came rushing up-stairs with some Christmas for the two girls. He was shocked beyond measure. He hardly dared go in and see Dil, but she called him in a weak, sad tone.

"O Dil!" That was all he said for many minutes, as he sat on the side of the cot, holding her hand. The strange look in her face awed him.

"Have ye seen Owny?" he whispered.

"Not since the night mother beat him."

"Owny—he's safe. He'll do well. Don't bodder yees poor head 'bout him. He's keepin' out o' der way, 'cause he's 'fraid de old woman'll set de cop on him. He ain't comin' back no more, but don't you worry. But he'll feel nawful! O Dil, I never s'posed she'd go so soon, if she was 'pindlin' an' weakly. Seemed when she'd lived so long—"

Patsey broke down there.

"O Patsey, I didn't s'pose she could die, jes' common dyin' like other folks. They've taken her away an' put her with dead people—I don't know where. You'll tell *him*. An'—an' mebbe 'twould be better if he didn't come back. Mother'd beat him nawful, and 'pears 's if I couldn't see any more beatin's. Don't tell me an' then I won't know. But you'll see an' keep him safe."

"Poor Dil! I'm jist as sorry's I kin hold. I loved you an' Bess, for I didn't never hev any folks," said the boy brokenly.

"An', Patsey, d'ye mind the wild roses ye brought in the summer? They was so sweet. She 'most went crazy over 'em with pure joy. An' that night she talked of thim, an' smelled thim, an' it was a bad sign. If I'd knowed, I might a done somethin', or had the doctor. An' she talked so beautiful—"

Dil was choked with sobs.

"Ye did iverything. Ye were like an angel. She wouldn't a lived half so long, but for yous. O Dil, I wisht I could bring her back. There was a boy tellin' 'bout some one—he heerd it at the Mission School—that jist took a man outen his coffin, an' made him alive. I'll ask him how it was, an' tell yous."

"Ye's so good, Patsey," with a weary sigh.

"An' I'll be droppin' in an' bring ye news. An' ye mustn't git sick, fer whin spring opens we'll spring a trap that'll s'prise ye. O Dil dear!"

He bent over and kissed her, his face all wet with tears. He had often kissed little Bess, though he was not "soft on gals." It was a solemn caress. Dil seemed so far away, as if he might lose her too.

The next morning the Christmas chimes rang out, and there were houses full of happy children making merry over Christmas gifts. The mission schools were crowded, the Christmas-trees and the feasts thronged. There were hundreds of poor children made happy, even if they could not take in the grand truth that eighteen hundred years ago a Saviour had been born to redeem the world. "Why is it not redeemed?" cried the cavillers, looking on. "If the truth is powerful, why has it not prevailed?" But the children amid their pleasures asked no questions.

Churches were full of melody, homes were full of joy and gladness, the streets in a tumult of delight; but Bessy Quinn was in her small grave, and Dil bitterly alone.

John Travis thought of them both this morning. "I hope Miss Nevins has planned a nice Christmas for them," he said to himself, since his Christmas in a foreign land was not as hopeful as he could wish. Perhaps Miss Nevins had found a way to Mrs. Quinn's heart. Women could sometimes do better than men.

Dilsey Quinn could not die; and if she was miserable and forlorn she had not the morbid brain to consider suicide, though she knew people had killed themselves. But the utter dreariness of the poor child's soul was overwhelming.

Still, she rose on Monday morning, did her work, and cared for the babies as usual. It seemed so cruelly lonesome with only her and Dan. Mrs. Murphy was very good to her, and begged her to go to the priest; but she listened in a weary, indifferent manner. If Bess was in purgatory, then she would like to go too. But in her heart she knew Bess wasn't. She was just dead, and couldn't be anywhere but in the ground.

She had never known any joyous animal life. Hers had been all work and loving service. There was nothing to buoy her up now, nothing to which she could look forward. She was too old, too experienced, to be a child, to share a child's trivial joys.

Her mother questioned her closely about Owen. Hadn't he never sneaked in for some clothes? Didn't Patsey know where he was?

"I'll ast him if he comes agen," she said, as if even Owen was of no moment to her. "He hasn't been here sence—sence that night."

"Ye's not half-witted, Dil Quinn, an' you grow stupider every day! Sometime I'll knock lightnin' outen yer! An' if ye dast to keep it from me that he kem'd home, I'd break yer neck, yer sassy trollope. He'll be saunterin' in some night, full o' rags, an' no place to go, an' there be a pairty, now, I tell ye!"

But Owny knew when he was well off. Dan went to school regularly, and was much improved.

After the holidays the winter was hard. Work fell off, and babies were slow coming in. Mrs. Murphy's little one took a severe cold, and was carried off with the croup. She gave up her rooms and went out to service. So poor Dil lost another friend.

One Sunday during the latter part of January, Dil summoned up pluck enough to go out for a walk. There had been three or four lovely days that suggested spring, bland airs and sunshine, and the indescribable thrill in the air that stirs with sudden longing.

Dil wandered over to Madison Square. Some one had given her mother a good warm cloak, quite modern. How Bess would have enjoyed seeing her dressed in it! But though the sun shone so gloriously, she was cold in body and soul, as if she could never be warm again. The leafless branches were full of swallows chirping, but the flowers were gone, the fountain silent. No one noted the solitary little figure sitting just where she had sat that happy afternoon.

"Oh," she cried softly, while her heart swelled to breaking, and her eyes wandered southward, "do you know that Bess is dead, an' we can't never go to heaven together as we planned? I d'know's I want to now. I jes' want to die an' be put in the ground. I wisht I could be laid 'long-side of her, an' I'd stretch out my arms, an' she'd come creepin' to them, jes' as she used. She'd know how to find me. An' when you come back you can't see her no more. Oh, 'f we only could 'a' started that day! An' mammy burned up Christiana an' my beautiful picture, so I'm all alone. There ain't nothin' left," and she sighed drearily.

Where was he? "'Crost the 'Lantic Oshin," as Bess had said. She had no more idea of the Atlantic Ocean than she had of the location of heaven; not as much, for it seemed as if heaven might be over beyond the setting sun. But John Travis was still in the world. And as she sat there it seemed as if she must live to tell him about Bess, and an aim brightened her dreary life. Two months and a little more. She would come over often when the weather grew pleasanter. Already she began to feel better.

But she could not take the heartfelt glow back to Barker's Court. The loneliness settled down like a pall. The long, long evenings were intolerable. Sometimes she crept down and spent an hour with Mrs. Minch; but she was afraid her mother might come home inopportunely.

Mrs. Quinn was growing much worse in her habits; and she lost her best place, which did not improve her temper. Dil's apathetic manner angered her as well; yet the house was kept cleaner than ever, her mother's clothes were always in order, and there was nothing to find fault about, except the lack of babies, which Dil could not help.

One night in February there was quite a carouse at Mrs. MacBride's. It was midnight when Mrs. Quinn returned. Poor Dil should have been in bed, out of harm's way; but she had been living over that fateful night, believing with the purest and most passionate fervor that she might have called Bess back to life if she could have gone to her.

A man helped Mrs. Quinn up the stairs, and tumbled her in the door. Dil sprang up in affright.

Mrs. Quinn stared at Dil with bleared eyes.

"What yer doin' up this time o' night? Yees do be enough to set wan crazy wid yer mewlin', pinched-up mug that's humbly as a stun! Why d'n' ye laugh an' hev a good time, an' make the house decent, stead er like a grave? I'm not goin' to stan' it—d'y hear?"

Dil glanced about in alarm, and would have fled to her room, but her mother caught her by the arm.

"Come," she cried, "I'll shake the glumness outen yer. Why, ye'd spile vinegar even! I'll tache ye a little friskiness."

Dil struggled to free herself, but uttered no word.

"I'll tache ye!" she shouted, the devil put into her by rum driving her to fury. "Ye measlin', grouty little thing! forever moanin' an' cryin' fer the sickly brat that's gone, good riddance to her! Come, now, step up lively. We'll make a night of it, an' ye shall hev a sup o' gin to wet yer t'roat whin ye get warm."

She whirled Dil about savagely, until she was dizzy and faint, and broke away in desperation. But her mother clutched her again, and gave her a resounding box on the ear. She managed, as she was whirled round, to open the door into the hall, and scream with all the strength she could summon. Her mother seized her again with a dreadful imprecation. What happened, how it happened in the dark, Dil could never clearly remember.

Fred Minch sprang up and opened the door. Something bumped down the stairs, and lay in a heap at his feet.

"It's that poor little girl, mother. She's bleeding, killed maybe. I'll run for a policeman."

Mrs. Minch picked up the senseless child. Mrs. Quinn went on yelling, swearing, smashing things, and dancing like a mad woman.

Rows were no uncommon thing in the court. Windows were thrown up. Who was it? Some wretched wife being beaten? And when they found it was Mrs. Quinn, they shook their heads. She had been going to the dogs of late, it was plain to see.

When the officer came, she made such a vigorous onslaught that he was forced to call assistance. She was after Owen now, and Dil had hidden him. The threats she uttered were enough to make one shudder. They mastered her at length, and dragged her down-stairs, where Mrs. Minch was waiting to explain poor Dil's plight.

She was still unconscious when the ambulance came. There was a bad cut up in the edge of her hair, but no bones seemed to be broken that any one could discover.

"Poor child!" said Mrs. Minch, when quiet was restored. "It would be a blessing if she could go with Bess. She'll never get over the loss. She's not been the same since, and many a day my heart's ached for her."

"She were a nice smart woman, that Mrs. Quinn, if she'd a let rum alone," was the general verdict. "An' though she took the child's death in a sensible manner, it broke her all up," said some of the court people, "and she went to hard drinking at once."

When Mrs. Quinn's trial came on, Dil's life was still hanging in a doubtful balance. She was sent to the Island for ninety days, for drunkenness and assaulting the policeman, and would there await the final result.

But Mrs. MacBride went on adding to her bank account and her real estate, to the wreck of youth and womanhood, to the prisons and paupers' graves. She kept such a very respectable place, the law never meddled with her.

Dilsey Quinn lay on her hospital pallet delirious, but never violent, and lapsing into unconsciousness. She had a dislocated shoulder, two broken ribs, and sundry bruises; but it was the years of hard work, foul air, dark rooms, and unsanitary conditions that the doctors had to fight against blindly. Her bruised and swollen face, her stubby, red-brown hair that had been cut short, her wide mouth and short nose, made no appeal in the name of beauty. She was merely a "case."

Her nurse was a youngish, kindly woman, used to such incidents. Beaten wives and children were often sent to her ward. In the early part of her experience she had suffered with them. Now she had grown—not unsympathetic, but wiser; tender she would always be.

Now and then there was something so wistful in the child's eyes that it touched her heart. She lay so patient and uncomplaining, she made so little trouble.

But sometimes the woman wondered why they were brought into the world to suffer, starve, and die. What wise purpose was served?

XI—WHEN HE AND SUMMER COMES

One morning Dilsey Quinn looked slowly and curiously around the ward, and then asked the nurse how she came there.

She lay a long while, piecing out the story, remembering what was back of it.

"As you did not die, your mother will come out of the Island early in June. I suppose it was a sort of accident. Was she used to beating you?"

A flush went over the pallid face.

"No," she replied quietly.

"Do you want to go back to her?"

"O, no, no!" with a note of terror in the voice. "I couldn't live with her no more."

"Have you any friends?"

There was a hesitating look, but the child did not answer. Had she any friend? Yes, Patsey.

"How would you like to go to some of the Homes? You would be well treated and taught some trade," the nurse ventured kindly.

"I can work for myself," returned Dil, with quiet decision. "I can keep house, an' tend babies, an' wash an' iron."

"Would you like a nice place in the country?"

"I want to stay in the city," she said slowly. "There's some one I want to see. It's 'bout my little sister that's dead. I can soon get some work."

"How old are you?"

"I shall be fifteen long in the summer, a spell after Fourth of July."

"You are very small. Are you quite sure?"

"Oh, yes. Why, you see, I was fourteen last summer. Jack was next to me. Then Bess. She was 'leven, but she hadn't grown any 'cause she was hurted."

"Hurt? How?" the nurse asked with interest. The children told their stories so simply.

"Along o' father's bein' nawful drunk an' slammin' her agin the wall. He went to prison 'cause he most killed a man. Bess died just before Christmas. We was goin'—"

Dil paused. Would nurse know anything about a journey to heaven?

"Were you going to run away? But if the poor little girl was hurt, she is better off. God is taking care of her in heaven."

"Oh, no. She isn't there. She's just dead. We was goin' together in the spring, and—and some one was going with us who knew all 'bout the way."

"My child, what do you know about heaven?" asked the nurse, struck by the confident tone.

"I didn't know—much. I heard 'bout it at the Mission School, and told Bess. We wanted to go like Christiana. We met a man in the square last summer, an' he told us 'bout his Lord Jesus, that he could cure little hurted legs that hadn't ever grown any and couldn't walk. An' he promised to go to heaven with us. We was goin' to start then, but we didn't just know the way. I'd learned 'bout the river in the Mission School. An' he said he'd bring us the book 'bout Christiana, an' then we'd know; but we better wait, for it would be so cold before we got there, an' the cold shrivelled up poor little Bess so. Well, we waited an' waited, but he did come, an' he brought the book. It was so lovely." Dil gave a long, rapturous sigh, and a glory shone in her eyes. "An' we found out 'bout crossin' the river an' the pallis. We see her goin' up the steps. An' then mammy took the book an' burnt it up in a tantrum, an' we couldn't read it any more, but we'd got the pictures all fixed in our minds. Curis, isn't it, how you can see things that ain't there, when you've got thim all fixed in your mind?"

"And you were going to heaven?" Nurse was amazed at the great, if misplaced, faith. "And your friend—"

The soft, suggestive voice won Dil to further confidence.

"He had to go 'way crost the 'Lantic Oshin. But he would have come back. He did just what he told you, always. An' that's why I must get well an' go back an' see him an' tell him—"

The voice faltered, and the eyes overflowed with tears. Dil's hearer was greatly moved.

"Bess has gone to heaven first, my poor dear," but her own voice was tremulous with emotion.

"Oh, she couldn't. Why, she couldn't walk, with her poor hurted legs, 'n' 'twas so cold 'n' all. An' she wouldn't 'a' gone to the very best heaven, not even the pallis shinin' with angels, athout me."

"But you don't understand"—how should she explain to the literal understanding. "The Lord came for her, took her in his arms, and carried her

101

to heaven."

"Oh, he wouldn't 'a' taken her athout sayin' a word, and leaved me behind, 'cause he must 'a' knowed we was plannin' to go together. No; she's just dead like other folks. An' *he* can't see her when he comes."

There was a long, dreary, tearless sob.

"Oh, my poor child, she *is* safe with the Lord. Do you really know who God is?"

"Mr. Travis's Lord Jesus lives in heaven," said Dil, in a kind of weary, half-puzzled tone. "He told us how he come down to some place, I disremember now, an' cured hurted people, an' made blind folks see, an' fed the hungry, an' went back an' fixed a beautiful pallis for them. There's lots more in Barker's Court that they swear by, but them ain't the ones Mr. Travis meant."

The nurse was as much astonished by the confident ignorance as Mr. Travis had been, and felt quite as helpless.

"I wish you could believe that little Bess is in heaven," she said gently.

"She couldn't be happy athout me," the poor child replied confidently, with tears in her faltering voice. "I always tended her, an' curled her hair, an' wheeled her about, an'—an' loved her so." The tone sank to a touching pathos. "An' she didn't go crost no river—she couldn't stand up 'thout bein' held. An' oh, do you s'pose I'd gone an' left Bess for anything? No more would she gone an' left me."

The brown eyes were heart-breaking in their trustful simplicity. The child's confidence was beyond any stage of persuasion. With time one might unravel the tangle in her untutored brain, but she could not in the brief while the child would remain in the hospital.

"Tell me about your friend, Mr. Travis," the nurse said, after a silence of some moments.

"He painted pictures, an' he made a beautiful one of Bess. But mammy burned it with the book. She said there wasn't any heaven anyway. An' Mrs. Murphy said it was purgatory, 'n' if you paid money, you'd get out. But Bess would go there. An' *he* didn't say nothin' 'bout purgatory. He come one day an' sang the beautifullest hymn 'bout 'everlastin' spring,' an' everybody cried. Poor old Mrs. Bolan was there. But when he comes back he'll tell me just how it is."

Perhaps that was best. Nurse went about her duties, the strange, sweet, entire faith haunting her. And the pathos of the two setting out for a literal heaven!

There were days when Dil sat in a vague, absent mood, her eyes staring into vacancy, seeming to hear nothing that went on about her. But she improved slowly; and though the nurse tried to persuade her to go to some friends of hers, she found the child wonderfully resolute.

And yet, when she was discharged, an awful sense of loneliness came over Dilsey Quinn. The nurse gave her a dollar, and an address to which she was to apply in case of any misfortune.

"You've been so good," Dil said, with swimming eyes. "An' I'll promise if I don't get no place."

And now she must find John Travis. He would surely know if Bess could get to heaven in any strange way, alone in the night. And if she was there, then Dil must go straightway. She could not even lose a day.

The world looked curious to her this April day. There were golden quivers in the sunshine, and a laughing blueness in the sky. And oh, such a lovely, fragrant air! Dil felt as if she could skip for very joy.

She found her way to the square, and sat down on the olden seat. Already some flowers were out, and the grass was green. The "cop" came around presently, but she was not afraid of him now. She rose and spoke to him, recalling the summer afternoon and the man who had made pictures of herself and Bess.

"I don't know who he was. No, he hasn't been back to inquire." The policeman would not have known Dil.

"His name was Mr. John Travis. He writ it on Bess's picture. I was so 'fraid I'd miss him. But he will come, 'cause he can't find no one in Barker's Court. An' when I get a place, I'll come an' bring the number, so's you can tell him."

"Yes, I'll be on the lookout for him." The child's grave, innocent faith touched him. How pale and thin she was!

Then she considered. Mrs. Minch would be in the court, she thought. Perhaps she might steal in without any one seeing her who would tell her mother afterward. And she could hear about Dan.

She stopped at a baker's, and bought some lunch. But by and by she began to grow very tired, and walked slowly, looking furtively about. She was almost at Barker's Court when a familiar whistle startled her.

"O Dil Quinn, Dil!" cried a dear, well remembered voice.

Patsey Muldoon caught her hand as if he would never let it go. He had half a mind to kiss her in the street, he was that glad. His eyes danced with joy.

"I've been layin' out fer ye, Dil, hangin' round an' waitin'. I was dead sure yous'd come back here. An' I've slipped in Misses Minch's, an' jes' asked 'bout the old gal, an' I told her 'f you come, jes' to hold on t'ye."

"O Patsey!"

"How nawful thin ye air, Dil. Have ye got railly well?"

Dil swallowed over a great lump in her throat, and had much ado not to cry, as she said, "I'm not so strong."

"Well, we want ye, we jes' do," and he laughed.

"What for?" It was so good to have any one want her in this desolation, that she drew nearer, and he put her hand in his arm in a very protecting fashion.

"Well, I'll tell ye. See, now, we was boardin' with an old woman. There was five of us, but Fin, he waltzed off. The old woman died suddint like three weeks ago, an' we've bin keepin' house sence. The lan'lord he come round, 'n' we promised the rent every Monday, sure pop; an' we paid it too," proudly. "We've got Owny. I've had to thrash him twict, but he's doin' fus' rate now. An' he sed, if we could git a holt o' yous! He said ye made sech lickin' good stews 'n' coffee 'twould make a feller sing in his sleep."

"O Patsey, you alwers was so good!" Dil wiped her eyes. This unlooked-for haven was delightful beyond any words.

"'Twas norful quair I sh'd meet you, wasn't it? An' we jes' won't let any one in de court know it, 'n' they can't blow on us. The ould woman's up on de Island, but her time'll soon be out. Dan, he's gone to some 'stution. We'll keep shet o' her. She's a peeler, she is! Most up to the boss in a shindy, now, wasn't she? But when dey begins to go to de Island, de way gits aisy fer 'em, an' dey keep de road hot trottin' over it."

Dil sighed, and shuddered too. We suppose the conscious tie of nature begets love, but it had not in Dil's case. And she had a curious feeling that she should drop dead if her mother should clutch her.

"I don't want to see her, Patsey, never agen. Poor Bess is gone—"

"Jes' don't you mind. My eyes is peeled fer de old woman! An' where I'm goin' to take you's so far off. But we'll jes' go an' hev some grub. We'll take de car. I'm out 'n a lark, I am!"

Patsey laughed, a wholesome, inspiriting sound. Dil was very, very tired, and it was so good to sit down. She felt so grateful, so befriended, so at rest, as if her anxieties had suddenly ended.

It was indeed a long distance,—a part of the city Dil knew nothing about,— across town and down town, in the old part, given over to business and the commonest of living. A few blocks after they left the car they came to a restaurant, and Patsey ordered some clam-chowder. It tasted so good to the poor little girl, and was so warming, that her cheeks flushed a trifle.

Patsey amused her with their ups and downs, the scrapes Owny had been in, and some of his virtues as well. Patsey might have adorned some other walk in life, from the possibilities of fairness and justice in his character.

Dil began to feel as if she belonged to the old life again. Her hospital experience, with the large, clean rooms, the neatness, the flowers, the visitors, and her kindly nurse, seemed something altogether outside of her own life.

They trudged along, and stopped at the end of a row of old-fashioned brick houses, two stories, with dormer windows. A wide alley-way went up by the last one. There was a building in the rear that had once been a shop, but now housed four families. Up-stairs lived some Polish tailors; at the lower end, a youngish married couple.

It was quite dusk now, but a lamp was lighted in the room. Two fellows were skylarking, but they stopped suddenly at the unusual sight of a "gal."

"Why it ain't never Dil!"

Owny was an immense exclamation point in supreme amazement.

"Didn't I tell yous! I was a-layin' fer her. An' she's jes' come out o' the 'ospital."

"Dil, you look nawful white."

"We'll make her hev red cheeks in a little, jes' you wait. This feller's Tom Dillon."

Dilsey took a survey of her new home, and for the first moment her heart failed her. It looked so dreadfully dirty and untidy. The room was quite large, with an old lounge, a kitchen table, a trunk, and some chairs; a stove in the fireplace, and a cupboard with the door swinging open, but the dishes seemed to be mostly on the table.

"We sleep here," explained Patsey, ushering her into the adjoining apartment. There was an iron bedstead in the centre of the room, and four bunks in two stories ranged against the side. "Ye see, we ain't much at housekeepin', but youse c'n soon git things straight," and Patsey laughed to hide a certain shame and embarrassment. "We'll clean house to-morrer, an' hev things shinin'. An' here's a place—"

It was a little corner taken off the other room, and partly shut in by the closet. "Th' ould woman used to sleep here—say, Dil, yous wouldn't be afraid—tell ye, a feller offered me a lot o' paper—wall paper, an' we'll make it purty as a

105

pink."

Dil had never seen "th' ould woman," and had no fear of her.

"It'll be nice when we get it fixed," she said cheerily.

Then Sandy Fossett came in, and was "introjuced." He, too, had heard the fame of the 'lickin' good stews,' but he was surprised to find such a very little body.

Dil lay on the lounge that night, but did not sleep much, it was all so strange. Any other body would have felt disheartened in the morning, but Patsey was "so good." He "hustled" the few things out of the little room, asked the woman in the other part about making paste, and ran off for his paper. Dil found a scrubbing-brush, and had the closet partly cleaned when he returned. Mrs. Brian came in and "gave them a hand." She was a short, stout, cheery body, with just enough Irish to take warmly to Dil.

If the poor child had small aptitude for book-learning, she had the wonderful art of housekeeping at her very finger ends. In a week the boys hardly knew the place. Dil's little room was really pretty, with its paper of grasses and field flowers on the lightest gray ground. She scalded and scrubbed her cot, and drove out any ghost that might have lingered about; she made a new "bureau" out of grocery boxes, not that she had any clothes at present, but she might have. She was so thankful for a home that work was a pleasure to her, though she did get very, very tired, and a pain would settle in the place where the ribs were broken.

The living room took on a delightful aspect. The chairs were scrubbed and painted, the table was cleaned up and covered with enamelled cloth. And such coffee as Dil made; such stews of meat and potatoes and onions, and a carrot or a bit of parsley; and oh, such soups and chowders! When she made griddlecakes the boys went out and stood on their heads—there was no other way to express their delight. Fin came back in a jiffy, and another lad, named Shorty by his peers. Indeed, there could have been ten if there had been room.

Owen was very much improved. He was shooting up into a tall boy, and had his mother's black eyes and fresh complexion. When the two boys talked about Bess, Dil could almost imagine her coming back. She sometimes tried to make believe that little Bess had gone to the hospital to get her poor hurted legs mended, and would surely return to them.

There was quite a pretty yard between the two houses. It really belonged to the "front" people. There was a grass-plot and some flowers, and an old honeysuckle climbing the porch. The air was much better than in Barker's Court, and altogether it was a more humanizing kind of living. And though the people up-stairs ran a sewing-machine in the evening, there were no rows. Mr. Brian did some kind of work on the docks, and went away early, coming back at half-past six or so. He was a nice, steady sort of fellow; and though he had protested vigorously against a "raft of boys" keeping house, after Dil came he was very friendly.

Patsey also "laid out" for Mrs. Quinn. When she came down from the "Island," she heard that her furniture had been set in the street, and then taken in by some of the neighbors. Dan was in a Home, Owen had not been seen, neither had Dilsey. Then the woman drank again and raged round like a tiger, was arrested, but pleaded so hard, and promised amendment so earnestly, that sentence was suspended.

It was well that Owen and Dilsey kept out of her way, for if she had found either of them she would have wreaked a full measure of vengeance upon them. There had never been a great deal of tenderness in her nature, and her experiences of the last ten years had not only hardened but brutalized her. The habit of steady drinking had blunted her natural feelings more than occasional outbreaks with weeks of soberness. She had no belief in a future state and no regard for it. Still, she had not reached that last stage of demoralization—she was willing to work; and when she had money to spend, Mrs. MacBride made her welcome again.

After Dil had her house a little in order, and had made herself a new gingham gown, she took her way one lovely afternoon over to Madison Square. She had meant to tell Patsey about John Travis, but an inexplicable feeling held her back. How she was coming to reach after higher things, or that they were really higher, she did not understand. Heaven was still a great mystery to her. With the boys Bess was simply dead, gone out of life, and sometime everybody seemed to go out of life. Why they did was the inscrutable mystery?

It was curious, but now she had no desire to finish Christiana, although she devoted some time every day to reading. The old things that had been such a pleasure seemed sacred to Bess, laid away, awaiting a mysterious solution. For she *knew* John Travis could tell her all about it.

Patsey had written her name and address on a slip of paper, several of them indeed, so as not to raise any suspicion. He laughed, and said she "was very toney, wantin' kerds." She saw the policeman, and was relieved that she had not missed Travis, yet strangely disappointed that he had not come.

The boys just adored her, and certainly they were a jolly lot. Sometimes they had streaks of luck, at others they were hard up. But every Saturday night the rent money was counted out to make sure, and the agent was soon greatly interested in her. She was a wonderful little market woman, and she found so much entertainment going out to do errands. She used to linger about the flower stands, and thrill with emotions that seemed strange indeed to her. She took great pleasure in watching the little flower bed a thin, delicate looking woman used to tend, that belonged to the front house.

One day Patsey brought her home a rose.

"Oh," she cried, "if Bess was only here to see!" and tears overflowed her eyes. "O Patsey, do you mind them wild roses the lady gev you an' you brought to us? They're always keepin' in my mind with Bess."

"I wisht I knew where they growed, I'd go fer some. But ain't this a stunner?"

"It's jes' splendid, an' you're so good, Patsey."

"I wisht yer cheeks cud be red as that," the boy said earnestly.

Mrs. Brian went out now and then to do a bit of washing, "unbeknownst to her man," who thought he earned enough for both of them. She came and sat on the little stoop with Dil occasionally, and had a "bit of a talk." Patsey had advised that she should let folks think both her parents were dead—he had said so in the first instance to make her coming with them seem reasonable.

But one day she told Mrs. Brian about little Bess, "who was hurted by a bad fall, and died last winter." Then she ventured on a wonder about heaven, hoping for some tangible explanation.

"I s'pose it's a good thing to go to heaven when you're sick, or old an' all tired out, but I ain't in any hurry. I want a good bit o' fun an' pleasure first. My man sez if you're honest an' do the fair thing, it's as good a religion as he wants, an' he'll trust it to take any one there. My 'pinion is that some of them that talks about it don't appear to know, when you pin 'em down to the pint. My man thinks most everybody who ain't awful bad'll go. There's some folks so dreadful you know, that the devil really ought to have 'em for firewood."

No one seemed in any hurry to go. It was a great mystery to Dil. And now Barker's Court seemed as if it must have been the City of Destruction. If only her mother had been like Christiana! It was all such a puzzle. She was so lonely, and longed for some satisfying comfort.

The weather was so lovely again. Ah! if Bess had not died, they would have started by themselves, she felt quite sure. And as the days passed with no John Travis, Dil sometimes grew cold and sick at heart. In spite of the boys' merriment and kindliness, she could not get down to the real hold on life. It seemed to her as if she was wandering off in some strange land, when she used to sit alone and wonder; it could hardly be called thinking, it was so intangible.

XII—THE RESPONSE OF PINING EYES

The boys chipped in one evening and took Dil to the theatre. They were fond of the rather coarse fun and stage heroics. Dil was simply bewildered with the lights, the blare of the second-rate orchestra, and the crowds of people. She was a little afraid too. What if they should meet some one who knew her mother?

A curious thought came to her unappeased soul. Some one was singing a song, one of the rather pathetic ballads just then a favorite. She did not see the stage nor the young man, but like a distinct vision the little room in Barker's Court was before her eyes. Bess in her old wagon, Mrs. Murphy with her baby in her arms, old Mrs. Bolan, and the group of listening women. The wonderful rapture in Bess's face was distinct. It was the sweet old hymn that she was listening to, the voice that stilled her longing soul, that filled her with content unutterable.

There was a round of applause that brought her back to the present life. They were rather noisy here. She liked the dreamland best.

"That takes the cake jist!" declared Patsey, looking down in the bewildered face. "What's the matter? Youse look nawful pale!"

"My head aches," she said. "It's so warm here. And it's all very nice, but will it be over soon, Patsey?"

The boy *was* disappointed; but the next morning Dil evinced such a cordial interest in all the points that had amused them, that Patsey decided that it must have been the headache, and not lack of appreciation.

But he hung around after the others were gone, with a curious sense of responsibility.

"Youse don't git reel well any more, Dil," he said, his voice full of solicitude. "Kin I do anythin'—"

"O Patsey!" The quick tears came to her eyes. "Why, I *am* well, an' everything's so nice now, an' Mrs. Brian jes' lovely. Mebbe I ain't quite so strong sence I was sick. An' sometimes I get lonesome with you away all day."

"I wish youse knowed some gals—"

"Patsey," a soft, tender light came to her brown eyes, "I think I miss the babies. They're so cunnin' an' sweet, an' put their arms round your neck an' say such pritty little words. An' if I could have some babies I wouldn't wash any more. That puts me out o' breath like, an' hurts my side. 'Twas that tired me for last night."

"Youse jist sha'n't wash no more, then. But babies is such a bother!"

"I love thim so. An' only two, maybe. Curis there ain't a baby in this house, nor in the front, neither. Babies would seem like old times, when I had Bess."

There was such a wistful look in her pale, tender face. Patsey thought she had grown a great deal prettier, but he wished she had red cheeks. And he was moved to go out at once and hunt up the babies.

Other girls might have made friends in the neighborhood; but Dil had never acquired friendly arts, and now she shrank from companionship. But she liked Mrs. Brian; and that very afternoon as they sat together Dil ventured to state her desires.

"You don't look fit to bother with 'em. You ought to be out pleasurin' a bit."

"But I'm strong, though; an' I used to be such a fat little chunk! I was stunted like; but I think I look better not to be so fat," she said with quaint self-appreciation.

"There's one baby I could get for you easy. The mother's a nice body—you see, the man went off. She's waitress in a restaurant, an' her little girl's pretty as a pink, with a head full of yellow curls, an' big blue eyes. She pays a dollar for her keep, 'ceptin' nights an' Sundays. An' you'd be so good, which the woman ain't. You couldn't hurt a fly if you tried."

"Oh, if I could have her!" cried Dil eagerly. A little girl with golden hair, curly hair. And a dollar would pay for the washing and ironing. The boys had been so good about fixing up things and buying her clothes that she had felt she must do all she could in return.

"I'll see about it this very evenin', dear."

"Oh, thank you! thank you!"

The mother, a slim young thing, came to visit Dil on Sunday, with pretty, chubby, two-year-old Nelly, who was not shy at all, and came and hugged Dil at once. Her prettiness was not of the *spirituelle* order, as Bess's would have been under any circumstances. The eyes were merry and wondering, the voice a gay little ripple, and comforted Dil curiously.

And through the course of the week several "incidental" ones came. It *was* like old times.

"Seems to me it's nawful tough to be nussin' kids," said Patsey; "but, Dil, you've chirked up an' grown reel jolly. You're hankerin' arter Bess, an' can't forgit. An' ef the babies make ye chipper, let 'em come. I only hope they won't take any fat offen yer bones, fer youse most a skiliton now. But sounds good to hear youse laugh agen."

"I'd like just a little fat in my cheeks," she made answer.

Patsey brought her home a white dress one day, and said they would all go down to Coney Island some Sunday.

"I wouldn't dast to," she said. "I'd be that afeared o' meetin' mother. She used to go las' summer. An' if she should find me—"

"Yer cudden't find anybody, les' yer looked sharp. An' youse er that changed an' sollumn lookin' an' big-eyed, no one'd know yer."

"But *you* knew me," with a grateful little smile.

Patsey grinned and rolled his eyes.

"I was a-layin' fer ye."

"You can take me up to Cent'l Park, Patsey. I'd like to go so much."

"That's the talk, now! So I will. We'll all go. We'll have a reg'lar persesh, a stunner, an' take our lunch, like the 'ristocrockery!"

Dil did brighten up a good deal. Baby kisses helped. She was starving for love, such as boys did not know how to give. She used to take Nelly out walking, and imagine her her very own. The mother instinct was strong in Dil.

Having the washing done did ease up the work; though one would have considered it no sinecure to feed five hungry boys. Now and then her head would ache, and occasionally something inside of her would flutter up in her throat, as it had when Bess died, and she would stretch out her hands to clasp some warm human support, her whole body in a shiver of vague terror.

If John Travis would only come. She *could not* disbelieve in him. Last autumn in the moment of desperate despair he had come, bringing such a waft of joy and satisfaction. There were so many things she wanted to ask him. She began to hope, in a vague way, that the Lord had come for Bess, for she wanted her in that beautiful heaven. But the mystery was too great for her untrained mind. And there intruded upon her thought, the horror of that moment when she knew Bess was dead.

The hot weather was very trying. Hemmed in on all sides by tall buildings, her own room so small, with a window on a narrow space hardly six inches from the brick wall of the next house, there was little chance for air. The boys seemed to sleep through anything.

So the weeks passed on with various small delights and events. The boys would go off and spend their money when they needed clothes, and then would follow heroic efforts at economizing. Dil had such shrewd good sense, and they did listen to her gentle advice. They were a gay, rollicking lot, but their very spirits seemed to be of a world she had passed by. It was as if she was on the way to some unknown land, not quite a stranger, but a sojourner.

Owen was a really tolerable boy, and bade fair to keep out of the reform school. They all mended of their swearing; they were ready to wait on her at a word.

The white frock was a beauty. Shorty brought her some pink ribbons that made her look less pale, and she had a wreath of wild roses on her hat that Mrs. Brian gave her.

They made ready for their excursion one beautiful Sunday morning in July. There had been a tremendous shower the night before, and all nature was fresh and glowing. The very sky was full of suggestions in its clear, soft blue, with here and there a white drift.

Oh, how lovely the park looked! Dil had to pause in a strange awe, as if she was hardly prepared to enter. It was like the hymn that was always floating intangibly through her mind—the fields and rivers of delight, the fragrant air, the waving trees and beds of flowers, the beautiful nooks, the bridges, the winding paths that seemed leading into delicious mysteries.

The boys were wild over the animals. They were irrepressible, and soon tired out poor Dil. She had to sit down and press her hand on her heart. There was a strange sinking, as if she was floating off, like the fleecy white drifts above her.

"Youse air nawful white!" cried Patsey in alarm. "An' ther's sich a queer blue streak acrost yer lip. Air ye sick?"

She drew a long breath, and the world seemed to settle again, as she raised her soft eyes with a smile all about them.

"No, Patsey—I'm only a bit tired. Let me sit an' get rested."

She took the sunbrowned hand in hers with a mute little caress that brought a strange flush to the lad's face.

"Youse jist work too hard wid dem babies an' all."

"I'm only going to have Nelly next week, an' the Leary baby is to go in the country with his mother to live. 'Twasn't nothin' but a queer flutt'rin' like, an' it comes sometimes in the night when I *can't* be tired. It's all over now;" and she looked bright and happy, if still pale.

Patsey seemed hardly satisfied.

"I think it's the hot weather. It's been so hot, you know. An' to-day's splendid! I'll get better when cool weather comes, I'm most sure. You an' the boys take a good long walk, an' I'll stay here with the lunch, an' get all rested up. An' I'll make b'leve it's heaven; it's so beautiful."

"See here, Dil, don't yer go an' be thinkin' 'bout—'bout heaven an' sich—"

Patsey swallowed over a big lump in his throat, and winked vigorously.

"Bess an' I used to talk about it," she said in a soft, disarming fashion. "We thought 'twas some-wers over the river there," nodding her head. "But I'll jes' sit still in some shady place, an' I won't go to-day," with a soft, comforting laugh.

The boys protested at first. But Dil had a way of persuading them that was quite irresistible. They were boys to the full, and to sit still would have half killed them. They found a lovely nook, where she could see the lake and the boats, and the people passing to and fro in their Sunday attire. There were merry voices of little ones that touched her like music.

She sat very still, with the lunch-basket at her feet. Occasionally some one cast a glance at the pale little girl in her white gown, with the wild roses drooping over the brim of her hat. A friendly policeman had seen the pantomime and the departure of the boys, and meant to keep guard that no one molested her.

Dil could understand being ill from some specific disease; but she did not feel ill, only tired. It was a different kind of fatigue from that back in Barker's Court, for then she could fall asleep in a moment. Now the nights were curiously wakeful. And the babies *were* heavy, even if there were only two of them.

The refreshing atmosphere and the tranquil, beautiful pictures all about her intensified the thought of the heaven she was going to "make b'leve" about. She could picture it out, up and up, through country ways and flowers, wild roses maybe. Houses where they took you in and fed you, and put you to bed in such soft, clean beds. Queer people too, who couldn't understand, and were wanting to turn back,—people who were afraid of lions and Giant Grim. She called up all the pictures she could remember, and they floated before her like a panorama.

"Though I can't get it out straight myself," and she sighed in helpless confusion. "I ain't smart as little Bess was, an' can't see into things. But I could push Bess along, an' Mr. Travis would be Mr. Greatheart for us, an' he'd know the way on 'count of his being book learned. An' we'd just be kerful an' not get into briars and bad places."

Was that Bess laughing softly, as she did sometimes when her poor back didn't hurt, and her head didn't ache. The sweet, lingering sound seemed to pervade the summer air. She could see the time-worn wagon, the rug made of odds and ends, that they had both considered such a great achievement. There was the sweet, pallid face, not quite as it had looked in those last days, but resembling more the beautiful picture that had gone to the flames, the crown of golden hair, the mysterious, fathomless eyes, with a new knowledge in them, that Dil felt had not been garnered in that old, pinched life.

Her own soul was suddenly informed with a mysterious rapture. She knew nothing of the Incarnation, of the love that came down and tasted pain and anguish, that others, in the suffering laid upon them, might also know of the joy of redemption. At that moment Dilsey Quinn was not far from the kingdom.

"O Bess! can't you come back?" she cried in a breathless, entreating manner, her eyes luminous with the rare insight of faith, the evidence of things unseen. "O Bess, you must be somewhere! I don't b'leve you died jes' like other folks! Can't you come back an' tell me how it happened, 'cause I know you wouldn't have gone and leaved me free of your own will?"

A tremendous longing surged at Dil's heart, and almost swept her away. Her breath came in gasps, her heart beat in great bounds, and then well nigh stopped. She was suddenly attuned to spiritual influences in that sweet, solemn solitude. Was it really Bess's voice in the softly penetrative summer air—was the strange, shadowy presence, so near that she could reach out and touch it—almost—that of the child?

She sat there rapt, motionless, seeing nothing with her mortal eyes; but in that finer illumination Bess moved slowly toward her, not walking, but floating, veiled in a soft, cloud-like drapery, stretching out her small, white hands. Dil took them, and they were not cold. She glanced into the starry eyes, and for moments that was enough.

"O Bess!" in the softest, tenderest whisper, "if you was in heaven I couldn't touch you, you'd be so far away. An' it's so sweet. But how did it all happen?"

"When *he* comes, an' I 'most know now that he will come soon, Bess, dear, he c'n tell me how to go to where you are—waitin', an' we'll start. There's somethin' I don't know 'bout, an' can't get straight. I never was real smart at ketchin' hold; but it's so beautiful to remember that his Lord Jesus took little children in his arms. An' mebbe he's took you up out o' the place they buried you, an' is keepin' you safe. You ain't there in the ground—you must be ris' up some way—"

The very birds sang of an unknown land in their songs; the wind murmuring gently through the trees thrilled her with an unutterable certainty. Her slow-moving eyes seemed to penetrate the very sky. Clear over the edge of the horizon it almost opened in its glory, as when Christiana was entering in; and she felt certain now that she should walk through its starry gates with Bess's little hand held tight in hers.

"O Bess, I c'n hardly wait for him to come! Seems as if I must fly away to where you be, but Patsey an' all the boys are so good to me. Seems if I never had such lovely quiet, an' no one to scold ner bang my poor head. But I want you so, Bess—"

She stretched out her hands, but the sweet form seemed to float farther off.

"O Bess, don't go away," she pleaded.

If the seers and the prophets saw heaven in their rapt visions, why not this poor starved little one whose angel always beheld the face of the Father in heaven. She was too ignorant to seize upon the truths of immortal life, but they thrilled through every pulse. She had no power of grasping any but the simplest beliefs, but she knew some love and care had sheltered Bess. The dawning of a knowledge that held in its ineffable beauty and sacredness the truths of resurrection penetrated her in a mysterious sense, aroused a faith that she could not yet comprehend; but it gave her a strange peace.

Her life had been a little machine out of which so much work must be steadily ground. It had needed all her attention. And Bess had taken all her love. But in the solitude and sense of loss she was learning to think.

Dil was startled when she saw the boys straggling along irregularly. How large and strong Patsey was growing! And how nice Owen looked in his clean summer suit! Oh, where was little Dan? She hoped he was happy, and had enough to eat and some time to play.

They were a hungry lot. The great pile of sandwiches disappeared in a trice. And the cake that an artist in cook-books might have disdained, the boys believed beat anything the best baker could turn out. There had never been any treat quite up to the cake. Of course the stew was more "fillin'" when one was tearing hungry, and cake was a luxury to their small income, but, oh, what a delight!

"You don't eat nothin," said Patsey, studying Dil anxiously.

"But I've rested so much. And I feel so happy."

There was a divine light shining in her eyes, and it touched the boy's soul.

"Dil, ef it wosn't fer them ere freckles right acrost yer nose, an' you wos a little fatter, you'd be jes' as pooty as they make 'em. Youse growed real han'some, only you want some red cheeks."

Dil colored at the praise. Did a light shine in her face because she had seen Bess? She would like to tell Patsey all about it. Yes, she had really seen her, but it was all infolded in mystery. How could she make it plain?

The boys ate up every crumb, and seasoned their repast with much merry jesting. Then they wanted to go on again. Wasn't Dil rested enough to go to the Museum?

It was a long walk, and after they entered Dil was glad to sit down. She looked at the curious white marble people, and asked Patsey if "they was truly people or dead folks." Shorty said "it was the mummies who were dead folks;" but Dil shuddered at the thought of Bess being like that. There were so many curious things, beautiful things, that the child was bewildered.

"'Tain't so nice as out o' doors," said Fin. "There's somethin' in the trees an' flowers, an' them places that are so still an' quiet like, that stirs a feller all up."

Rough and unlearned as they were, nature appealed to them powerfully. Ah, what a day it was!

"I've never had but just one time in my life that was so lovely," said Dil with sweet gratefulness: "an' that wasn't so beautiful, only strange. If anybody was so runnin' over full o' happiness all the time, 'pears to me it would kinder choke them all round the heart, so's they couldn't live."

"Don't know 'bout that," and Patsey chuckled. "Happy people ain't dyin' off no faster'n other people, an' don't commit suicide so easy. But, golly! 'twould take a good deal to fill a feller up chock full o' happiness, 'cause it's suthin' like ice-cream, keeps meltin' down all the time, 'n' youse can pack in some more."

"I jes' wish we had some now!" cried Owen, referring to the cream.

"It's been—well—super splacious! There ain't no word long ernuff to hold all's been crowded in this ere day," cried Fin enthusiastically. "Say, boys, why don't we come agin? Only ther's music days—an golly! I jes' wish I had lots of money an' a vacation. Vacations ain't no good when you don't have money."

Dil enjoyed their pleasure. She was so strangely happy. She had seen Bess, and some time the puzzle would be explained. She had taken her first lesson in faith, and she felt light and joyous, as if she could fly. The very air was full of expectation.

It was time to return, unless, indeed, they had brought their suppers along. Dil appreciated the long ride home. She was very tired, but the joy within buoyed her up.

There was the rather well-gleaned ham bone and a dish of potatoes for supper, and the last of the wonderful cake, which they stretched out, and made to go all around. And they seasoned the supper with jests and pleasant laughs, and plans of what they would do, and hopes of being rich some day. Dil listened and smiled. They were all so good to her!

When they were through, Patsey began to pile up the dishes and carry them to the sink. He often did this for Dil, and none of the boys dared chaff him. She rose presently.

The room, the very chair on which she rested her hand, seemed slipping away. All the air was full of feathery blue clouds. There was a curious rushing sound, a great light, a great darkness, and Dil was a little heap on the floor, white as any ghost.

Patsey picked her up in his arms, and screamed as only a boy can scream,—

"Run quick for some one. Dil's dead!"

XIII—THE LAND OF PURE DELIGHT

Owen started out of the door in a great fright. Mrs. Wilson was strolling in her yard, and the boy called to her. There was a side gate that led out in the alley-way. She came through quickly, although she had held very much aloof from these undesirable neighbors.

They had laid Dil on the lounge, stuffed anew and covered with bright cretonne. Patsey looked at her, wild-eyed.

"I think she has only fainted. My sister faints frequently." She began to chafe Dil's hands, and asked them to wet the end of the towel, with which she bathed the small white face, and the brown eyes opened with a smile, a little startled at the stranger bending over her. She closed them again; and Mrs. Wilson nodded to the intensely eager faces crowding about, saying assuringly,
—

"She will be all right presently."

Then she glanced around the room. It was clean, and it had some pretty "gift pictures" tacked up on the whitewashed wall. There was a bowl of flowers on the window-sill. The table had a red and white cloth, there were some Chinese napkins, and cheap but pretty dishes. The long towel hanging by the sink was fairly sweet in its cleanliness, and this pale little girl was the housekeeper!

"Have you ever fainted before? What had you been doing?" she asked in a quiet manner.

"We'd been up to Cent'l Park. It was so beautiful! But I guess I got tired out," and Dil smiled faintly. "You see, I was in the hospital in the spring, an' I ain't so strong's I used to be. But I feel all well now."

"Youse jes' lay still there, 'n' Owny, 'n' me'll wash up the dishes."

Patsey colored scarlet as he said this, but he stood his ground manfully.

"They're so good to me!" and Dil looked up into her visitor's eyes with such heartsome gratitude that the lady was deeply touched. "Patsey," she added, "you've got on your best clo'es, 'n' I wish you'd tie on that big apern. Mrs. Wilson won't make fun, I know."

"No, my child; I shall honor him for his carefulness," returned Mrs. Wilson.

Patsey's face grew redder, if such a thing was possible, but he tied on the apron.

"I ought to have been more neighborly," began Mrs. Wilson, with a twinge of conscience. "I've watched you all so long, and you have all improved so much since old Mrs. Brown was here! But everybody seems so engrossed with business!"

"That's along o' Dil," put in Patsey proudly. "When Dil come things was diff'rent. Dil's got so many nice ways—she allis had."

"Is your mother dead?"

Dil's face was full of scarlet shame and distress, but she could not tell a wrong story.

"Her mother ain't no good," declared Patsey, in his stout championship; for he did not quite like to tell a lie, himself, to the lady, and he knew Dil wouldn't. "But Dil's splendid; and Owny, that's her brother," nodding toward him, "is fus' rate. We're keepin' together; an' little Dan, he's in a home bein' took keer of."

"O Patsey!" Dil flushed with a kind of shamefaced pleasure at his praise.

"So you be! I ain't goin' back on you, never." And there was a little gruffness in his voice as is apt to be the case when a lump rises in a big boy's throat. "An' you couldn't tell how nice she's fixed up the place—'twas jes' terrible when she come."

"But you all helped," returned Dil.

"And you are all so much cleaner and nicer," and their visitor smiled.

"Yes; we'm gittin' quite tony." Patsey slung out the dishcloth and hung it up, and spread the towel on a bar across the window. Fin and Shorty edged their way out, and Fossett settled to a story paper. Owny wanted to go with the boys, but he compromised by sitting in the doorway.

"There is a little child here through the week, and I've seen a baby. My child, you are not compelled to care for them, are you?"

"We didn't want her to," protested Patsey; "but you see, there was another pooty little thing, her sister Bess, who was hurted 'n' couldn't walk, 'n' Dil took care of her. 'N' las' winter she died, 'n' Dil's been kinder broodin' over it ever sence. We wos off all day, 'n' she got lonesome like; but she ain't gonter have 'em any more, 'cause she ain't strong, 'n' we kin take keer of her," proudly.

"You look as if you ought to be taken care of altogether for a while."

Mrs. Wilson studied the pale little face. It had a curious waxen whiteness like a camellia. The eyes were large and wistful, but shining in tender gratitude;

the brows were finely pencilled; the hair was growing to more of a chestnut tint, and curled loosely about her forehead. She was strangely pretty now, with the pathetic beauty that touches one's heart.

"Tell yer wot, Dil, us fellers'll chip in an' save up a bit 'n' send youse off to the country like the 'ristocrockery. You don't happen to know of some nice, cheapish place?" and Patsey glanced questioningly at the visitor.

"There are very nice places where it doesn't cost anything. Country people often take children for a fortnight or so. My daughters went to a beautiful seaside place last summer that a rich lady fitted up for clerks and shop-girls. Of course they are older than you, young ladies, but—let me think a bit—"

Mrs. Wilson had never known much besides poverty. Youth, married life, and widowhood had been a struggle. She hired the whole front house, and rented furnished rooms to young men whose incomes would not afford luxurious accommodations. Her sister was in poor health; her two girls were in stores. Her son, who should have been her mainstay and comfort, was in an insane asylum, the result of drink and excesses.

"I can't remember, but I must have heard my girls talking about places where they take 'little mothers,'—the children who tend babies, and give them a lovely holiday in a beautiful country place, where they can run about the green fields and pick flowers and play and sing, or sit about and have nothing to do. I will try to learn something about them."

"I don't b'leve I could go 'way," said Dil, with soft-toned doubtfulness.

"I wish you'd talk her out'n havin' any babies. She ain't no ways strong 'nuff. An' we boys kin take keer o' her. She airns her livin' over 'n' over agin. She's had 'nuff to do wid kids all her life," protested her champion.

"But Nelly's so sweet, and 'companies me so much," Dil said longingly.

"But you orter be chirkin' up a bit, 'stead er gittin' so thin, an' faintin'. 'Twas nawful, Dil. You looked jes' 's if youse wos dead."

"It didn't hurt any, Patsey;" and she smiled over to him. "'Twas queer like 's if all the bells in the world was ringin' soft an' sweet, an' then you went sailin' off. 'Twas worse when I went to ketch my breath afterward. But I'm all right now."

She glanced up smilingly to Mrs. Wilson, who took the soft little hands in hers, for soft they were in spite of the hard work they had done. Patsey had whisked the table up to the side of the room and brushed up the crumbs. Then he sat down and watched Dil.

Mrs. Wilson said she must go in home, but she would run over in the morning. Patsey expressed his thanks in a frank, boyish manner, and Dil's eyes said at least half of hers.

Then Mrs. Brian and her husband returned, and she stopped to hear what kind of a picnic they had had. Between the three they told all the story and the fright.

"Yes; she must give up all but Nelly, for her mother wouldn't know how to stand it on such a short notice. The child achilly cries for you on Sundays, her mother told me. But we can't have you killed for any babies in the land," said Mrs. Brian emphatically.

"That's the talk!" exclaimed Patsey.

"Why, I feel jes' as well as ever, an' all rested like," and Dil sat up, smiling. "We walked so much to-day, but to-morrow I'll be all right."

She seemed quite right the next morning. When Mrs. Brian's "man" had gone, she came in and helped Dil with the breakfast things. Mrs. Cairns *would* leave her baby for the half-day, and Nelly came. Mrs. Wilson looked in upon her, with a bit of sewing in her hand. Dil did not try to do anything besides entertain the little ones. How sweet and naturally she did it!

But she was so tired she lay on the lounge a long while in the afternoon. Nelly played about, and talked in her pretty broken fashion. Dil dreamed of the vision she had seen.

About five Mrs. Wilson came in, her thin face lighted with eagerness.

"I must tell you something quite delightful," she began. "I sew for several ladies; and one of them, a Miss Lawrence, came in about an hour ago. She's interested in several charities, and I asked her about the places where they sent poor tired children to recruit. My dear, she is on the committee of a society; and they have a beautiful large country-house, where they can take in from twenty to thirty children. There's a housekeeper and nurses, and different young ladies go up to stay a week or two at a time. They read to the children, and take them out in the woods, and help them at playing games; and there are music and singing, and great shady trees to sit under, and a barn full of new-mown hay, where they can play and tumble. Why, it made me wish I was a little girl!"

Mrs. Wilson put her hand on her side, for she had talked herself out of breath.

Dil's eyes shone with delight. She could see it all in a vivid manner.

"Miss Lawrence couldn't stay to-day; but she is coming to-morrow morning, and wants to see you. She was so interested in the way all you children are living here. She's a lovely woman; and if there were more like her, who were willing to pay fair prices for work, the poor would be much the gainer."

"You're so good to me! Everybody is now," said the child gratefully.

Dil thought she hadn't done much of anything that day, but she was really afraid to tell Patsey how tired she felt. He *would* wash up the dishes.

"That'll be jes' the daisy, Dil!" he said, when he heard about Miss Lawrence. "You want some country air, an'—an' reel fresh country milk. An' don't you worry. We'll git along. You jes' go an' hev a good time."

Oh, could she go to such a blessed place—like Central Park all the time?

She was quite shy and embarrassed when Miss Lawrence called. A large, pleasant-looking woman, with indications of wealth and refinement that Dil felt at once, and she seemed so much farther away than Mrs. Wilson. But she questioned Dil very gently, and drew her out with a rare art. The pale face and evident weakness appealed to her,—seemed, indeed, to call for immediate attention.

"I shall put you on our next week's list," Miss Lawrence said with gracious interest. "If any one ever earned a rest, I think you have. And I will come in to-morrow evening and talk it over with your brother and the boys."

The "boys" made themselves scarce, except Patsey and Owen, although Shorty went and sat on Mrs. Brian's stoop. But Miss Lawrence had seen boys before, and even ventured on a dainty bit of slang that won Patsey at once. He was eager for Dil to go and get some red cheeks like Owen. It didn't seem as if the two could be brother and sister.

If Miss Lawrence had seen the sleeping accommodations she would have been more than shocked; and yet there were hundreds in the city not as well housed, and few of the real poor as tidily kept.

"It would be jes' lovely to go," admitted Dil, with curious reluctance. "But a whole week!"

"Two weeks!" almost shouted Patsey. "An' youse'll come home so fat wid de new milk an' all, yer clo'es won't fit yer. We'll jes' hev to make an auction an' sell em' second-hand."

"An' take half the money an buy her some new ones," said Owen with a laugh. "T'other half we'll put in the bank."

Shorty had come sneaking back, and joined in the merriment.

"'N' I kin cook purty good, 'n' wash dishes," began Patsey, when Dil interrupted,—

"Oh, you will be careful of thim, won't you?"

"Careful! I'll treat 'em as if they was aiggs. An' I'll make the boys stan' roun', so's to keep the house—well—decent!" and he made a funny, meaning face. "Je-ru-sa-lem! what a hole we had when youse come! An' now it's like a pallis."

Not like the palace Dil remembered in the book that had been such a treat to her and Bess.

Everybody made it easy for Dil. Mrs. Brian would see to the boys, and Mrs. Wilson offered to keep Nelly until her return. Still, it was Friday before Dil could really make up her mind.

On Saturday Dil took Nelly and went up to Madison Square. The policeman kept out of her way; he could not bear to face her look of disappointment. But just at the last she took him inadvertently.

"You see, I'm sure he'll come soon," she said with a confidence that seemed like a presentiment. "'Cause he'll be thinkin' 'bout the Sat'day he made the picture of Bess an' me. An' I want him to know where I've gone; so I've writ it out. I've been studyin' writin'."

"She looks like a ghost," the man said to himself as his eyes followed her. "She's that changed in a year no one would know her except for her eyes. If he don't come soon, he won't see her at all, to my thinking. Hillo! what a scheme! I'll hunt him up. Why didn't I think of it before! John Travis! Seems to me I've heard something about John Travis."

Sunday was a soft, cloudy day, with a touch of rain. Every boy stayed at home —you couldn't have driven them away. They promised to give Mrs. Brian the rent every night, so as to be provided for next Monday. They sang some of their prettiest songs for her; they didn't know many hymns, but they had a spirit of tenderest devotion in their hearts.

The boys said good-by to her the next morning in a rather sober fashion. Patsey and Owen were going to take her to the ferry. Mrs. Brian brought down her satchel, and Dil put in her white dress, some aprons, and various small matters. She was to wear her best pink gingham. Mrs. Wilson was full of hope, Mrs. Brian extremely jolly, and was sure Barnum would want her for a "fat girl" when she came back.

Dil's similitudes were very limited, but Cinderella and the fairy godmother *did* come into her mind.

Miss Lawrence was in the waiting-room with half a dozen girls. She came and greeted Dil cordially, and told her she looked better already. The child's eyes brightened with a sunny light.

Owen said good-by in a boy's awkward fashion, and gave her the bag. Patsey was reluctant, and he turned slowly away.

Then he came back.

"Good-by, Dil, dear," he said again with deep tenderness as he stooped to kiss her. He was so much taller, though only a few months older. And always Patsey Muldoon was glad he came back for that kiss.

Then Miss Lawrence bought tickets and ushered her small procession, nine of them now, through the narrow way and out on the boat. They huddled together at first like a flock of sheep. Dil noticed one little hump-backed girl, who had large, light eyes and golden hair in ringlets. She was not like Bess, and yet she moved Dil's sympathetic heart. Had a drunken father "hurted her"?

She felt shy of the others, they all seemed in such spirits. As they were going off the boat, she drew nearer the unfortunate child and longed to speak.

An impudent leer crossed the other face.

"Who yer lookin' at? Mind yer own biz. I'm jes' as good as youse!" was the unexpected salutation.

"Yes," answered Dil meekly, her enthusiastic pity quenched.

Dil's seat was in the window end, and her companion a stolid little German with two flaxen tails down her back. So she sat quite still. The morning had been so full of excitement she could hardly think. She had been just whirled about, pushed into the adventure.

But the "little mothers" interested her. Did they like babies, she wondered? Did their arms ache, and were their backs strained and tired carrying them about? Most of them were thin and weary looking, yet they were in gay spirits, making little jokes and giving quick, slangy answers, ready to laugh at anything.

Dil seemed quite apart from them. They passed through a tunnel, and there were little shrieks and giggles. The German girl caught Dil's arm. Then they crossed rivers, passed pretty towns, bits of woods, flower gardens, long fields of waving corn, meadows where daisies still lingered, and tufts of red clover looked like roses. Ah, how large the world was! And maybe heaven was a great deal farther off than she and Bess had imagined. They might have been all winter going if they had walked. She felt suddenly thankful that John Travis had advised against it.

It was Dilsey Quinn's first railroad journey, and it gave her the sensation of flying. She had brightened up, and a soft flush toned the paleness. An indescribable light hovered about her face, the rapt look that we term spiritual.

They trooped out of the train,—it seemed a week since they had started, her brain was so full of beautiful impressions. A young lady had come down to meet them, and walked with Miss Lawrence. The children were wild with the newness of everything; some of them had not even seen the nearest park before. They chased butterflies; they longed to chase the birds; they ran and laughed, and presently came to a great white house set in an old orchard.

"Children," said Miss Lawrence, "here is your new home. You can run and play to your heart's content. In the woods yonder you can shout and be as wild as you like. But you must come in first and take off your best dresses. And now you must mind when you are spoken to, and not quarrel with each other."

They went through a wide hall and up an old-fashioned staircase. Three large rooms were full of narrow white-draped cots. The girls who pushed on ahead were given numbers to correspond. There were pegs for their hats and garments, a shelf for their satchels and bundles. What a whispering, chattering, and giggling! Here was a bath-room, and basins for washing. And then the bell rang for dinner.

Oh, what a dinner it was to most of the newcomers! A great slice of sweet boiled beef, vegetables, and bread in an unstinted fashion, and a harvest apple for dessert. Dil was too full of rapture to eat, and she let the next girl, whose capacity seemed unlimited, have most of her dinner.

Afterward they went out to play. Hammocks and swings were everywhere. They ran and shouted. They sat in the grass, and laughed with a sense of improbable delight. No one to scold, no work to do, not to be beaten for a whole long week! Oh, what joy it was to these little toilers in courts and slums and foul tenement houses!

Dil sat on a seat built around a great tree, and watched them. She was like one in a dream, quite apart from them. There is a delightful, unquestioning freemasonry among children. The subtle sign is given in a word or look or smile, and they are all kin. But it had been so long since Dil was a child, that she had forgotten the language.

She was not unhappy nor solitary. She was simply beyond playing, far from boisterous mirth. She had been doing a woman's work so long, and childhood for the poor is ever a brief season.

Two or three girls shyly asked her to play "tag." She gently shook her head. Then a long-ago sound caught her attention.

Two little girls were holding their clasped hands up as high as they could stretch. A small procession passed, each girl holding to the skirt of the other, and singing:—

"Open the gates as high as the sky,
And let King George and his men go by.

Needle's eye as I pass by,
Awaiting to go through;
Many a lass I have let pass,
And now I have caught you."

Down came the arms of the "gates" over the head of the girl just under them. There was a shriek and a giggle. Then the one who was caught had to be a "gate," and so it went on.

Dil looked, fascinated with a kind of remembered terror. It seemed as if she must have heard that in another world, it was so long, long ago. Before Bess was "hurted," when Dan was a chubby baby, she had them both out, caring for them. At least, Dan was in the corner of the stoop, and Bess was tossing a ball for his amusement. A group of girls were playing this very game. The arms came down and took Dilsey Quinn prisoner, and all laughed because she had been so quick to evade them.

Something else—her mother's heavy hand that dragged Dil out of the ring. The girls scattered, afraid of the tall, strong virago. Dil picked up the baby and took Bess by the hand. They were not living in Barker's Court then. She shuddered, for she knew what awaited her. She should have been in the house, getting supper, to be sure. She had not meant to play so long, and even then she so seldom played.

Poor Dil! For a fortnight or so she carried the marks on her body.

"I'll tache ye to be wastin' of yer time foolin' wid sich," said her mother.

Then Bess was "hurted," and her mother ill in bed for weeks. They were warned out of the house, and for some time it was hard lines for them all. Dil never played any more. Childhood was at an end for her.

And when she heard the merry voices here, a cold, terrible shiver came over her with the old memories. Was it softened by the thought that Bess could run about then? But even little Bess had sometimes been cruelly beaten. After that —was there a strange comfort that had never come before, that Bess's accident had saved her many an unreasonable punishment? For Mrs. Quinn had let the poor little sufferer pretty much alone. Dil had managed to stand between, and take the blows and ill usage.

Does God note all the vicarious suffering in the world, and write it in the book of remembrance?

Dil turned her head away. Another party were playing "Ring a round a rosy." And a group on the grass were being inducted into the mystery of "Jacks." She wondered a little where her mother was. She did not want to see her, but she hoped matters were better with her. Surely she need not work so hard. And oh, if she would not drink gin! But Dil had noted the fact that most women did as they grew older.

Miss Lawrence came out presently with a bright cheery word for them all.

"You're not playing," she said to Dil. "You must run about and have some fun, and get some color in your cheeks. And you must not sit and brood over your hard life. That is all passed, and we hope the good Father has something better in store. And you must be friendly with the others."

"Yes'm," answered Dil, with soft pathos. "Only I'd rather sit here an' look on."

"Don't get homesick after your boys," and the lady's smile went to Dil's heart. "You'll feel less strange to-morrow. I want this outing to be of real benefit to you. I'm going down to the city now, and will see Mrs. Wilson. When I come again I'll bring you some word from the boys. I am sure everything will be done for your comfort."

"Yes'm," Dil answered meekly, but with an uplifted smile.

Several little girls ran and kissed her a rapturous good-by. When Dil saw her go out of the gate she felt strangely alone. She wanted to fly home to the boys, to get their supper, to listen to their merry jests and adventures, to see their bright eyes gleam, and hear the glad laughter. She felt so rested. Oh, if she had *not* promised Patsey to stay a whole long week. And one day was not yet gone.

She espied a vacant hammock, and stole lightly out from her leafy covert to take possession. It was odd, but the little hump-backed girl seemed a centre of attraction. She said so many droll, amusing things. She was pert and audacious to be sure. She could talk broken Dutch and the broadest Irish, and sing all the street songs. The children were positively fascinated with her. A wonder came to Dil as to how it would feel to be so enthusiastically admired.

She lay there swinging to and fro until the supper bell rang long and loud. One of the attendants came and talked with her while the children were tripping in from the woods. Something in her appearance and gentle manner reminded Dil of the hospital nurse.

There was a good deal of singing in the evening, but they all went to bed early. How wonderfully quiet it was! No dogs barking, no marauding cats wauling dismally on back fences, no rattle and whiz of "L" cars, no clatter of heavy wagons. And oh, the wonderful sweetness in the air! If Dil had ever achieved Bible reading, she would have thought of "songs in the night" and a "holy solemnity," but she could feel the things unutterable.

The window was next to her bed. She sat up and watched the ships of fleece go drifting by. How the great golden stars twinkled! Were they worlds? and did people live in them? They made a mysterious melody; and though she had not heard of the stars singing for joy, she felt it in every pulse with a sweet, solemn thrill of rapture.

Was that heaven back of the shining stars? And oh! would she and Bess and John Travis be together there? For he would help her to call back Bess, as she came on Sunday. It was only a little while to wait now. She felt the assurance —for the poor ignorant little girl had translated St. Paul's sublime, "By faith."

The moon silvered the tree-tops, and presently sent one slant ray across the bed. Dil laid her hands in it with a trance of ecstasy. The delicious state of quietude seemed to make her a part of all lovely, heavenly things. It was the "land of pure delight" that John Travis sang about. A whole line came back to her,—

"And pleasures banish pain."

Dilsey Quinn had attained to the spiritual pleasures. Pain was not, could not be again.

She was not a bit sleepy. She watched the moon dropping down and down. All the insects had stopped. A soft darkness seemed spread over everything, and by dozens the stars went out. Ah, how wonderful it all was! If people could only have chances to know!

"My child," said Miss Mary at the breakfast table, "you are not eating anything! Don't you like porridge, and this nice milk?"

"Yes, it's so good," replied Dil gratefully. "An' the milk seems almost as if 'twas full of roses, it's so sweet. But I can't get hungry as I used, an' when I eat just a little I seem all filled up."

"Would you like bread better? And some nice creamed potatoes?"

"I don't want nothin' more." Dil looked up with a soft light in her eyes. "Mebbe by noon I'll be hungry—I most know I will."

"Yes, I hope so."

It was such a long morning to Dil, so hard to sit round and do nothing. If there had been a baby to tend, or a room to tidy. She would have been glad to go to the kitchen and help prepare the vegetables. She was so used to work that she could not feel at home in idleness.

She went over to the woods with the children to please Miss Mary, who suggested it so gently. But some feeling—the long disuse of childhood—held her aloof. She could not join in their plays, but it was a pleasure to watch them. And how wonderful the woods were! The soft grasses with feathery heads, the mosses, some of them with tiny red blossoms not as large as a pin's head. There were a few wild flowers left, and long trails of clematis wandering about; shining bitter-sweet, green chestnut burrs in clusters, the long, fringy blossoms in yellow brown still holding on to some of them. There were bunches of little fox grapes, too bitter and sour for even children to eat.

She sat down on a stone and almost held her breath. It was the real, every-day country, not Central Park. The birds sang at their own sweet will, and made swift dazzles in the sunshine as they flew from tree to tree. Could heaven be any better? But there was no pain nor sickness nor weariness in heaven. And she felt so strangely tired at some moments.

She used her utmost endeavors to eat some dinner. It had such an appetizing flavor. The little girl next to her, who had swallowed her supper so quickly last night, eyed it longingly.

"You can have the potato and the meat," Dil whispered softly. That travelled down red lane, and still seemed to leave a hollow behind. It was like the hungry boys at home, and she smiled.

She sat under the tree again, and Miss Mary tried to persuade her to go and play, but she was gently obstinate.

"Miss Lawrence asked me specially to look after her," she said to another of the attendants. "She looks like a little ghost; but whether she is really ill, or only dead tired out, I can't decide. It's so natural for children to want to play, but she doesn't seem to care to do anything but mope. Yet she speaks up so cheerful."

"Poor children! How hard some of their lives are," and her companion sighed.

Dil's supper tasted good; and she was so sorry she couldn't eat more, as she glanced up and caught Miss Mary's eye.

"I'm ever so much better," she said in her soft, bright manner. "I'm glad; for the boys wanted me to get well an' fat, an' have red cheeks. I'll try my best, you're all so good. An' it's such a beautiful place. I wonder what made— some one—think 'bout the little mothers? But the babies ought to be here too."

"That wouldn't give the little mothers much rest. Are there many babies in your family?"

"There ain't any, but—but some that come in. Other people's babies."

"And does your mother keep a nursery?"

"I ain't got any mother now. I took the babies 'cause I liked them."

"But where do you live?"

"With my brother an'—an' the boys. I keep house."

How unchildishly reticent she seemed. And most of the children were ready to tell everything.

The little household was called in for their evening singing.

XIV—VIRGINIA DEERING

Wednesday's visitor was a tall, slim girl with an abundance of soft, light hair, that fell in loose waves and dainty little curls. Her gown was so pretty, a sort of grayish-blue china silk with clusters of flowers scattered here and there. Her wide-brimmed, gray chip hat was just a garden of crushed roses, that looked as if they might shake off.

There was a charm about her, for the children who had seen her the week before ran to her with joyful exclamations. They kissed her white hands, they caught hold of her gown, and presently she dropped on the grass and they all huddled about her. She told them a story, very amusing it must have been, they laughed so. Sadie Carr, the little deformed girl, seemed to lay instant claim to her.

Dil had a strange, homesick yearning to-day. She longed so to see the boys. Her eyes overflowed with tears as she thought of them and their warm, vital love. She seemed almost to have lost Bess. Could she see her again at Cent'l Park she wondered? She would ask Patsey to take her there as soon as she went home.

A great hay wagon had come and taken a load of the children down to the meadows. Three were in disgrace for being naughty, and had to spend an hour sitting on the stoop. Some were reading. The German girl was crocheting.

Dil sat out under the old branching apple-tree, whose hard red apples would be delightful along in the autumn. She was counting up the days. To-night they would be half gone. Would they let her go on Saturday she wondered? She looked at her poor little hands—they hadn't grown any fat.

"Who is that little girl? and why does she keep apart from the others?" asked Miss Deering.

"I don't know. She seems strange and hard to get on with. But she looks so weakly that even sitting still may do her good. Go and see what you can make of her, Miss Virginia."

Miss Deering had several roses in her hand. She sauntered slowly down to Dil, and dropped the roses in her lap on the thin white hands.

"Oh, thank you!" Dil exclaimed gravely. She did not pick them up with the enthusiasm Miss Deering expected.

"Don't you care for flowers?" Miss Deering seated herself beside the quiet child, and studied the face turned a little from her.

"Yes, I like thim so much," glancing at them with a curiously absent air. Her manner was so formal and old-fashioned, and she roused a sense of elusiveness that puzzled the young lady.

"I think I must have seen you before. I can't just remember—"

Dil raised her soft brown eyes, lustrous still with the tears of longing that were in them a moment ago. The short curved upper lip, the tumbled hair, the gravely wondering expression—how curiously familiar it seemed.

"I hope you are happy here?" she said gently.

"I like it better home," Dil returned, but with no emphasis of ungraciousness. "I'm used to the boys, 'n' they're so good to me. But they wanted me to come an' get well. I wasn't reel sick only—Patsey don't like me to look like a skiliton, he says. Everybody here's so nice."

"And who is Patsey—your brother?"

She seemed to study Virginia Deering in her turn. It was a proud face, yet soft and tender, friendly. It touched the reticent little soul.

"No; Owen's my brother. There's some more boys, an' we keep house. Patsey is—Patsey's alwers been good to me an' Bess."

There was a touching inflection in her tone.

"Who is Bess?" with a persuasive entreaty that found its way to the lonely heart.

"Bess is—Bess was"—The voice trembled and died out. Virginia Deering slipped her arm about the small figure with a sympathetic nearness. Dil made another effort.

"Bess was my poor little hurted sister. I didn't ever have no other one."

"Don't you want to tell me about her? I should so like to hear. How did she get hurt?"

Virginia Deering had of late been taking lessons in divine as well as human sympathy. She was willing to begin at the foundation with the least of these.

Dil looked across the sunny field to the shaded, waving woods. There had never been any one to whom she could tell all of Bess's story. Mrs. Brian, tender and kindly, had not understood. A helpless feeling came over her.

"I wonder if she loved roses? Did she ever have any?" Miss Deering laid her finger on those in Dil's hand, then felt under and clasped the hand itself.

Dil was suddenly roused. The grave face seemed transfigured. Where had she seen it—under far different auspices?

"She had some wild roses wunst. Oh, do you know what wild roses is? I looked in the woods for some yest'day."

Wild roses! She had set herself to bear her lot, bruised and wrecked in an evil moment, with all the bravery of true repentance.

"Yes," in a soft, constrained tone. "I have always loved them. And last summer where I was staying there were hundreds of them."

"Oh," cried Dil eagerly, "that was jest what *he* said. It was clear away to las' summer. Patsey was up to Grand Cent'l deepo'. He carried bags an' such. An' a beautiful young lady gev him a great bunch. Casey made a grab fer thim, but Patsey snatched, an' he's strongest, 'n' he gev it to Casey good till a cop come, 'n' then he run all the way to Barker's Court an' brought thim to Bess an' me."

"A great bunch of wild roses! Oh, then I know something about Patsey. It was one day in August. And—and I had the roses."

Dil's face was a rare study. Virginia Deering bent over and kissed it. Then the ice of strangeness was broken, and they were friends.

This was Patsey's "stunner." She was very sweet and lovely, with pink cheeks, and teeth like pearls. Dil looked into the large, serious eyes, and her heart warmed until she gave a soft, glad, trusting laugh.

"Patsey'll be so glad to have me find you! They were the beautifullest things, withered up some, but so sweet. Me an' Bess hadn't never seen any; an' I put them in a bowl of water, an' all the baby buds come out, an' they made Bess so glad she could a-danced if she'd been well, 'cause she used to 'fore she was hurted, when the hand-organs come. They was on the winder-sill by where she slept, an' every day we'd take out the poor dead ones. 'N' there was jes' a few Sat'day when we went up to the Square an' met the man. 'N' I allers had to wheel Bess, 'cause she couldn't walk."

"What hurt her?"

"Well—pappy did. He was dreadful that night along a-drinkin', an' he slammed her against the wall, an' her poor little hurted legs never grew any more. An' the man said jes' the same as you,—that he'd been stayin' where there was hundreds of thim, an' he made the beautifullest picture of Bess— she was pritty as an angel."

Miss Deering's eyes fell on the little trail of freckles across Dil's nose. They were very small, but quite distinct on the waxen, pale skin.

"And he painted a picture of you! He put you in that wild-rose dell. I know now. I thought I must have seen your face."

Dil looked almost stupidly amazed.

"Bess was so much prittier," she said simply. "*Do* you know 'bout him? He went away ever so far, crost the 'Lantic Oshun. But he said he'd come back in the spring."

She lifted her grave, perplexed eyes to a face whose wavering tints were struggling with keen emotion.

"He couldn't come back in the spring. He went abroad with a cousin who loved him very much, who was ill, and hoped to get well; but he grew worse and weaker, and died only a little while ago. And Mr. Travis came in on Monday, I think."

Her voice trembled a little.

"Oh, I knew he would come!" The glad cry was electrifying.

And she, this little being, one among the waifs of a big city, had looked for him, had a right to look for him.

"He ain't the kind to tell what he don't mean. Bess was so sure. An' I want to ast him so many things I can't get straight by myself. I ain't smart like Bess was, an' we was goin' to heaven when he come back; he said he'd go with us. An' now Bess is dead."

"My dear little girl," Virginia held her close, and kissed the cool, waxen cheek, the pale lips, "will you tell me all the story, and about going to heaven?"

It was an easy confidence now. She told the plans so simply, with that wonderful directness one rarely finds outside of Bible narratives. Her own share in the small series of tragedies was related with no consciousness that it had been heroic. Virginia could see the Square on the Saturday afternoon, and Bess in her wagon, when she "ast Mr. Travis to go to heaven with them." And the other time—the singing. Ah, she well knew the beauty and pathos of the voice. How they had hoped and planned—and that last sad night, with its remembrance of wild roses. Dil's voice broke now and then, and she made little heart-touching pauses; but Virginia was crying softly, moved from the depths of her soul. And Dil's wonderful faith that she could have brought Bess back to life bordered on the sublime.

"Oh, my dear," and Virginia's voice trembled with tenderness, "you need never doubt. Bess *is* in heaven."

"No," returned Dil, with a curious certainty in her tone, "she ain't quite gone, 'cause I've seen her. We all went up to Cent'l Park, Sunday week ago. I was all alone, the boys goin' off walkin', an' me bein' tired. I wanted her so much,

I called to her; an' she come, all beautiful an' well, like *his* picture of her. I c'n talk to her, but she can't answer. There's a little ketch in it I can't get straight, not bein' smart like to understand. But she's jes' waitin' somewheres, 'n' he kin tell me how it is. You see, Bess wouldn't go to heaven 'thout me, an' he would know just where she is. For she couldn't get crost the river 'n' up the pallis steps 'les I had hold of her hand. For she never had any one to love her so, 'n' she wouldn't go back on me for a whole world."

Miss Deering could readily believe that. But, oh, what should she say to this wonderful faith? Had it puzzled John Travis as well?

"And who sent you here?" she asked, to break the tense strain.

Dil told of the fainting spell, and Mrs. Wilson and Miss Lawrence, who had been so good.

"But now he's come, you see, I must get well an' go down. He'll be there waitin'. I'd like to stay with the boys, but somethin' draws me to Bess. I feel most tore in two. An' ther's a chokin' in my throat, an' my head goes round, an' I can't hardly wait, I want to see her so. When I tell Patsey and Owny all about it, I'm most sure they'll want me to go, for they know how I loved Bess. An' when *he* comes, he'll know what's jes' right."

They were silent a long while. The bees crooned about, now and then a bird lilted in the gladness of his heart. Virginia Deering was asking herself if she had ever loved like this, and what she had suffered patiently for her love. For her self-will and self-love there had been many a pang. But she let her soul go down now to the divinest humiliation. Whatever *he* did henceforth, even to the dealing out of sorest punishment, must be right evermore in her eyes.

The children were coming back from their ride, joyous, noisy, exuberant; their eyes sparkling, their cheeks beginning to color a little with the vivifying air and pleasurable excitement. Dil glanced at them with a soft little smile.

"I think they want you," she said. "They like you so. An' I like you too, but I've had you all this time."

"You are a generous little girl." Virginia was struck by the simple self-abnegation. "I will come back again presently."

She did not let the noisy group miss anything in her demeanor. And yet she was thinking of that summer day, and the poor roses she had taken so unwillingly. How she had shrunk from them all through the journey! How she had tossed them out, poor things, to be fought over by street arabs. They had come back to her with healing on their wings. And that John Travis should have seen them, and the two little waifs of unkind fortune. Ah, how could *she* have been so fatally blind and cruel that day among the roses? And all for such a very little thing.

What could she say to this simple, trustful child? If her faith and her beliefs had gone outside of orthodox lines, for lack of the training all people are supposed to get in this Christian land, was there any way in which she could amend it? No, she could not even disturb it. John Travis should gather in the harvest he had planted; for, like Dil, she believed him in sincere earnest. She "almost knew that he meant to set out on the journey to heaven," if not in the literal way poor, trusting little Dil took it. And she honored him as she never had before.

She came back to Dil for a few moments.

"Don't you want to hear about the picture?" she asked. "It quite went out of my mind. Mr. Travis exhibited it in London, and a friend bought it and brought it home. I saw it a fortnight ago. So you brought him a great deal of good fortune and money."

"I'm so glad," her eyes shone with a soul radiance; "for he gev us some money—it was for Bess, an' we buyed such lots of things. We had such a splendid time! Five dollars—twicet—an' Mrs. Bolan, an' she was so glad 'bout the singin'. But I wisht it had been Bess. He couldn't make no such beautiful picture out'n me. Bess looked jes' 's if she could talk."

"He put you in that beautiful thicket of roses." Ah, how well he had remembered it! "I do not think any one would have you changed, but you were not so thin then."

"No;" Dil gave the soft little laugh so different from the other children. "I was quite a little chunk, mammy alwers said, an' I don't mind, only Patsey wants me to get fatter. Mebbe they make people look beautifuller in pictures," and she gave a serious little sigh.

Then the supper-bell rang. Dil held tightly to the slim hand.

"They're all so good," she said earnestly. "But folks is diff'rent. Some come clost to you," and she made an appealing movement of nearness. "Then they couldn't understand 'bout me an' Bess—that she's jes' waitin' somewheres till I kin find out how to go to her, an' then he'll tell us which way to start for heaven. I'm so glad you know *him*."

Dil tried again to eat, but did not accomplish much. She was brimful of joy. Her eyes shone, and a happy smile kept fluttering about her face, flushing it delicately.

"You have made a new child of her," said Miss Mary delightedly. "I thought her a dull and unattractive little thing, but such lives as theirs wear out the charms and graces of childhood before they have time to bloom. We used to think the poor had many compensations, and amongst them health, that richer people went envying. Would any mother in comfortable circumstances change her child's physique for these stunted frames and half-vitalized brains?"

Virginia Deering made some new resolves. It was not enough to merely feed and clothe. She thought of Dilsey Quinn's love and devotion; of Patsey Muldoon's brave endeavor to rescue Owen, and keep him from going to the bad, and his generosity in providing a home for Dil, to save her from her brutalized mother. Ah, yes; charity was a grander thing,—a love for humanity.

Dil came to say good-night. Virginia was startled by the unearthly beauty, the heavenly content, in her eyes that transfigured her.

"You breathe too short and fast," she said. "You are too much excited."

"I d'n' know—I think it's 'cause *he's* comin'. 'N' I've waited so, 'n' now it's all light 'n' beautiful, 'n' I don't feel worried no more."

"You must go to sleep and get rested, and—get well." Yes, she *must* get well, and have the different kind of life Virginia began to plan for her.

A soft rain set in. There was such a tender patter on the leaves that Dil almost laughed in sympathetic joy. Such delightful fragrance everywhere! For a moment she loathed the city, and it seemed as if she could not go back to the crowded rooms and close air. But only for a little while. John Travis would set her on the road to heaven.

It was curious how bits of the hymn came back to her. She could not have repeated the words consecutively—it was like the strain of remembered melody one follows in one's brain, and yet cannot give it voice. She seemed actually to *see* it.

"O'er all those wide extended plains,
    Shines one eternal day."

Eternal day! and no night. Forever to be walking about with Bess, when the Lord Jesus had taken her in his arms and made her like other children. Oh, did Sadie Carr know that in heaven she would be straight and nice and beautiful? She must ask Miss Deering to tell her. Then her heart went out with trembling, yearning tenderness toward her mother. Couldn't the Lord Jesus do something to keep her from drinking gin and going up to the Island? Was little Dan in a happy home like this, with plenty to eat?—boys were always hungry. She used to be before Bess went away, but it seemed as if she should never be hungry again.

The little girls around her were breathing peacefully. They were still well enough to have a good time when beneficent fortune favored. They had run and played and shouted, and were healthily tired. Dil remembered how sleepy she used to be when she was crooning songs to Bess. But since the day at Central Park it had been so different. The nights were all alight with fancies, and she was being whirled along in an air full of music and sweetness.

Toward morning it stopped raining. Oh, how the birds sang at daylight! She dropped off to sleep then, but presently something startled her. She was back with the boys, and there was breakfast to get. She heard the eager voices, and sprang out of bed, glancing around.

It was only the children chattering as they dressed. Perhaps she looked strange to them, for one little girl uttered a wild cry as Dil slipped down on the floor a soft little heap.

The nurses thought at first that she was dead, it was so long before there was any sign of returning animation, and then it was only to lapse from one faint to another.

"We must have the doctor," said Miss Mary. "And we will take her to my room. There are three children in the Infirmary, one with a fever."

The room was not large, but cheerful in aspect. A tree near by shut out the glare of the sunshine, and sifted it through in soft, changeful shadows.

"She looks like death itself. Poor little girl! And Miss Lawrence was so interested in her. Will you mind staying a bit, Miss Virginia? There are so many things for me to do, and the doctor will be in soon."

Virginia did not mind. She had been keeping a vigil through the night. She had taken a pride in what she called shaping her life on certain noble lines. How poor and small and ease-loving to the point of selfishness they looked now! What could there ever be as simply grand and tender as Dilsey Quinn's love for her little sister, and her cheerful patience with the evils of a hard and cruel life?

She had been in the wrong, she knew it well. She had waited for him to make an overture; but he had gone without a word, and that had heightened her anger. Then had come a bitter sense of loss, a tender regret deepening into real and fervent sorrow. Out of it had arisen a nobler repentance, and acceptance of the result of her evil moment. She had hoped some time, and in some unlooked-for way, they would meet.

But since she had given the offence, could she not be brave enough to put her fate to the touch and

"Win or lose it all"?

The words that had always seemed so hard to say came readily enough, as she told the story of the human blighted rose that had brought a new faith to her.

Dil seemed to rally before the doctor came. She opened her eyes, and glanced around with the old bright smile.

"It's all queer an' strange like," she said; "but you'm here, an' it's all right. Did I faint away? 'Cause my head feels light an' wavery as it did that Sunday night."

"Yes, you fainted. But you are better now. And the doctor will give you a tonic to help you get well. We all want you to get well."

"I ain't never been sick, 'cept when I was in the hospital, hurted. I only feel tired, for I ain't got no pain anywhere, an' I'll soon get rested. 'Cause I want to go down home an' see *him*. If I *could* go over to the Square on Sat'day. I 'most know he'll be waitin' for me."

Should she tell the poor child? Oh, was she sure John Travis would come? He need not see *her*. She had not asked for herself.

The kindly, middle-aged doctor looked in upon them at this moment, accompanied by Miss Mary. Dil smiled with such cheerful brightness that it almost gave the contradiction to her pale face. He sat down beside her, counted her pulse, talked pleasantly until she no longer felt strange, but answered his questions, sometimes with a shade of diffidence when they reflected on her mother's cruelty, but always with a frank sort of innocence. Then he listened to her breathing, heart and lungs, and the spot where the two ribs were broken, "that hadn't ever felt quite good when you rubbed over it," she admitted. He held up her hand, and seemed to study its curious transparency.

"So you are only a little tired? Well, you have done enough to tire one out, and now you must have a good long rest. Will you stay here content?" he asked kindly.

"Everybody's so good!" and her eyes shone with a glad, grateful light. "But I'd like to go by Sat'day. There's somethin'—Miss Deerin' knows"—and an expectant smile parted her lips.

"Well, to-day's Thursday, and there's Friday. We'll see about it. I'd like you to stay in bed and be pretty quiet—not worry—"

"I ain't got nothin' to worry 'bout," with her soft little laugh. "It's all come round right, an' what I wanted to know most of all, I c'n know on Sat'day. I kin look out o' the winder and see the trees 'n' the sunshine, an' hear the birds sing. An' everybody speaks so sweet an' soft to you, like 's if their voices was makin' music. O no, I don't mind, only the children'll want Miss Deerin', and I want her too."

"Your want is the most needful. She shall stay with you."

The brown quartz eyes irradiated with luminous gleams.

"Very well," he said, with an answering smile.

Miss Deering came out in the hall. He shut the door carefully.

"If she wants anything or anybody, let her have it. Keep her generally quiet, and in bed. Though nothing can hurt her very much. It is too late to help or hinder."

"O surely you do not mean"—Miss Deering turned white to the very lips.

"She's as much worn out as a woman of eighty ought to be. If you could look at her, through her, with the eye of science, you would wonder how the machinery keeps going. It is worn to the last thread, and her poor little heart can hardly do its work. Her cheerfulness is in her favor. But some moment all will stop. There will be little suffering; it *is* old age, the utter lack of vitality. And she's hardly a dozen years old."

"She is fifteen—yes, I think she is right, though I could hardly believe it at first."

"That poor little thing! I hope with all my soul there is a heaven where the lost youth is made up to these wronged little ones. She has been doing a woman's work on a child's strength."

"O can nothing save her?" cried Virginia Deering, with longing desire. "For her life might be so happy. She has found friends—"

"It all comes too late. If you should ever be tempted to reason away heaven, think of her and hundreds like her, and what else shall make amends? I will be in again this afternoon," and he turned away abruptly.

He met Miss Mary in the lower hall, and left her amazed at the intelligence. She came up-stairs and found Virginia with her eyes full of tears.

"And I thought last night she looked so improved. It is so sudden, so unexpected."

"How long?" asked Virginia, with a great tremble in her voice.

"Any time, my dear. A day or two, an hour may be. We must keep it from the children. So many have improved, and no one has died. I can't believe it."

"I want to stay with her," the girl said in a low tone.

"We shall be so grateful to you. You young girls are so good to give up your own pleasures, and help us in our work."

Virginia went back quietly. Dil's face was turned toward the window, and she was listening to the children's voices, as they ran around tumultuously.

"They do be havin' such a good time," she said, with a thrill of satisfaction in her tone.

"I wish you were well enough to join them," Virginia replied softly.

Dil laughed. "I've been such a big, big girl this long time," she returned with a sense of amusement, but no longing in her tone. "I don't seem to know 'bout playin' as they do; for mammy had so many babies, an' Bess was hurted, an' there wasn't never no room to play in Barker's Court, 'count o' washin' an' such. 'Pears like I'd feel strange runnin' an' careerin' round like thim," and she made a motion with her head. "I'd rather lay here an' get well. Oh, do you think the doctor'll let me go on Sat'day?"

"My dear, I have written to Mr. Travis. I think he will be up then."

"Oh!" Such a joyful light illumined the face, that Virginia had much ado to keep the tears from her own eyes. "You're so good," she said softly. "Everybody's so good."

"And the children don't disturb you?"

"Oh, no; I like it. I c'n jest shut my eyes 'n' see 'Ring around a rosy.' Oh," with a long, long sigh, "Bess would 'a' liked it so! I'm so sorry she couldn't come 'n' see it all, the beautiful flowers 'n' trees 'n' the soft grass you c'n tumble on 'n' turn summersets as they did yest'day. Don't you s'pose, Miss Deerin', there'll be a whole heaven for the children by themselves? For *he* told me somethin' 'bout 'many mansions' the Lord Jesus went to fix for thim all. Ain't it queer how things come to you?"

XV—JOHN TRAVIS

She lay there quietly all the morning, little Dilsey Quinn, trying in her hopeful fashion to hurry and get well. It was nicer than the hospital, and Miss Deering was so sweet, as she sat there crocheting some lovely rose-wheels out of pale-blue silk. Now and then some sentences flashed between them, and a soft little laugh from Dil. Miss Deering felt more like crying.

The doctor came about three.

"I'm most well," said Dil, with her unabated cheerfulness. "Only when I raise up somethin' seems tied tight around me here," putting her hand to her side. "'N' you think I c'n be well on Sat'day, cause—some one might come—"

"Are you expecting a visitor?"

"Miss Deerin' knows. An' he's one of the sure kind. Yes; he'll surely come. An' if I stay in bed all day to-day, don't you s'pose I'll be well to-morrow?"

"We'll see. You and Miss Deering seem to be planning secrets. I shall have to look sharp after both of you. And who brings you flowers?"

"Miss Mary. An' some custard, an' oh, Miss Deerin' fed me like as if I was a baby."

"That's all right. It's high time you were waited on a little. But I'd like you to take a nap. Miss Deering, couldn't you read her to sleep?"

"I will try."

"She ought to sleep some," studying the wide eyes.

"But I'm not a bit sleepy. I'm thinkin' 'bout when *he* comes, an' how he'll help me find Bess."

"It is astonishing," the doctor said down-stairs. "She has some wonderful vitality. It seemed this morning as if she couldn't last an hour, and now if she wasn't all worn out she might recover. But it is the last flash of the expiring fire. Is there some friend to come?"

"Yes," answered Miss Deering with a faint flush.

"She will live till then. If, she suffers we must try opiates, but we will hardly need, I think."

"And—the excitement—"

"She will not get excited. She is strangely tranquil. Do not disturb her serene hope, whatever it is."

The day drew to a close again. Dil asked if she was not going to her own bed, and seemed quite content. Miss Mary came in early in the evening and sent Virginia to bed. She could not quite believe the dread fiat. For Dil might be made so happy in the years to come. Ah, God, must it be too late? It seemed like the refinement of cruelty.

She came back about midnight, but Miss Mary motioned her away, and then went out in the hall.

"You must go to bed in earnest," she said. "You may be needed more later on. She is very quiet; but she lies there with her eyes wide open, as if she were seeing visions. I get a nap now and then; you see, I'm used to this kind of work."

"I wish 'twas mornin'," Dil said toward early dawn. "I want to hear the birds sing an' the children playin'; they do laugh so glad an' comfortin'. An' I wisht there could be some babies tumblin' round in the sweet grass. They'd like it so. Don't you *never* have any babies?"

"There are other homes for babies," was the reply.

"Do you s'pose it'll ever get all round,—homes, an' care, an' joy, an' such? There's so many, you know. There was little girls in Barker's Court who had to sew, an' never could go out, not even Sundays. When 'twas nice, Bess an' me used to go out on Sat'days. But the winter froze her all up. And the other poor children—"

"They will all get here by degrees."

"It's so good in folks to think of it."

"My dear, you must go to sleep."

"But I don't feel sleepy," and Dil's face was sweet with her serene smile. "There's so many lovely things to think about."

"Try a little, to please me."

Dilsey shut her eyes and lay very still. Was there some mysterious change in the face?

And so dawned another morning. Virginia Deering came in with a handful of flowers, which she laid beside Dilsey's cheek on the pillow.

"Oh," the child began in a breathless sort of way, "do you think he'll be here to-morrow, Sat'day? Cause I don't b'l'eve I'd be well 'nuff to go down. I don't seem to get reel rested like. An' you'll have to send word to Patsey. He wanted me to stay a good long while, an' get fat, an' I want to try."

Did *she* feel sure John Travis would come? Ah, she would *not* doubt. She would take the child's sublime faith for her stay. Even if he had ceased to care for her, he would not disappoint the child who relied so confidently upon his word.

"Yes, I know he will come."

"It'll be all right, then. An' I'll get up to-morrow an' be dressed, an' go downstairs all strong an' rested like. An' I think he'll know about Bess."

Virginia bent over and kissed her.

"Ain't the children jealous 'cause you stay here so much?" she asked presently. "They all like you so. An' they was so glad to see you."

"They do not mind," she made answer to the unselfish child; "and I like to stay with you."

"Do you? I'm glad too," she said dreamily.

But now and then she was a little restless. The doctor merely looked at her and smiled. But outside he said to Miss Mary, "I doubt if she goes through another night."

"What shall I do for you?" Virginia asked later on. There seemed such a wistfulness in the eyes turned to the window.

"It's queer like, but seems to me as if Bess was comin'. P'raps she's jes' found out where I be. O Miss Deerin', are there any wild roses? I'd like to have some for Bess."

Virginia glanced up in vague alarm.

"I think if I had some Bess would come back. 'N' I'm all hungry like to see her."

Dil moved uneasily, and worked her fingers with a nervous motion.

"There have been some over back of the woods there," and Miss Mary inclined her head. "There were in June, I remember."

"I might go and see."

"Oh, will you? I wisht so I had some."

"The walk will do you good." There had come a distraught look in Virginia's face. Oh, what if John Travis failed! Even to-morrow might be too late.

"You'll let the children go with you," said Dil. "They'll like it so; an' I'll keep still 'n' try to go to sleep."

The old serenity came back with the smile. She had learned so many lessons of patience and self-denial in the short life, the grand patience perfected through love and sacrifice, the earthly type of that greater love. But the sweet little face almost unnerved Virginia.

The children hailed her with delight, and clung so to her gown that she could hardly take a step. Perhaps it was their noise that had unconsciously worn upon Dil's very slender nerves. Miss Mary read to her awhile, and in the soft, soothing silence she fell asleep.

Yes, she had come to that sign and seal indelibly stamped on the faces of the "called." The dread something no word can fitly describe, and it was so much more apparent in her sleep.

"Miss Mary," said an attendant, "can you come down a moment?"

She guessed without a word when she saw a young man standing there with a basket of wild roses. But he could not believe the dread fiat at first. She had been "a little ill," and "wasn't strong" were the tidings that had startled him, and she had gone to a home for the "Little Mothers" to recruit. He had heard some other incidents of her sad story, and he remembered the children's pathetic clinging to the wild roses. Nothing could give her greater pleasure.

He walked reverently up the wide, uncarpeted steps, beside Miss Mary. Dil was still asleep, or—O Heaven! was she dead? Miss Mary bent over, touched her cool cheek.

Dil opened her eyes.

"I've been asleep. It was so lovely. I'm all rested like—why, I'm most well."

"Well enough to see an old friend?"

Oh, the glow in her eyes, the eager, asking expression of every feature. She gave a soft, exultant cry as John Travis emerged from Miss Mary's shadow, and stretched out her hands.

"My dear, dear little Dil!"

All the room was full of the faint, delicious fragrance of wild roses, kept so moist and sheltered they were hardly conscious of their journey. And she lay trembling in two strong arms, so instinct with vitality, that she seemed to take from them a sudden buoyant strength.

"I've been waitin' for you so long," she exclaimed when she found breath to speak. There was no reproach in the tone, rather a heavenly satisfaction that he had come now. Her trust had been crowned with fruition, that was enough.

"My little girl!" Oh, surely it could not be as bad as they said. The future that he had planned for, that he had meant to make pleasant and satisfying, and perhaps beautiful, from the fervent gratitude of a manly heart. Was she beyond anything he could do for her? Oh, he would not believe it!

"I was detained so much longer abroad than I expected," he began. "And we did not get in until Monday morning. I went to Barker's Court, and could not learn where you were. Then I bethought myself of the cop at the square," smiling as he designated the man.

"An' he gev you my letter?"

"He gave me the letter. I hunted up the boys. I saw Patsey and Owen last night, and they are counting on your getting well. They sent you so much love. And to-day I went to Chester. Here are your roses."

He tumbled them out all dewy from the wet papers. Oh, such sweetness! Dil breathed it in ecstatic delight. She had no words. She looked her unutterable joy out of her limpid brown eyes, and he had much ado to keep the tears from his. So pale, so spiritualized, yet so little like Bess, and—oh, the last hope died as he took in all the signs. For surely, surely she was on the road to heaven and Bess. No hand of love, no touch of prosperity, could hold her back.

"'Pears like everything's come, an' there ain't nothin' left to wish for," she said as he laid her down again, and watched the transfigured face. "For now you c'n tell me 'bout Bess. Mother burned up the book one day, an' we never could quite know, only she got crost the river, an' they was all so glad at the pallis. An' Bess was so sure you'd come. The cough was dreadful when we didn't have some good medicine that helped her. An' the lady come one afternoon, 'n' mammy was home 'n' she was norful sassy to her. You see, we hadn't dast to tell mammy—"

"My poor child!" He was toying with the soft, tumbled hair. He had heard another side of the story, and of Mrs. Quinn's insulting impudence.

"An' then Bess she smelt the wild roses all around one night, an' thought she was gettin' better—an'—an' she jus' died."

"Yes; God came for her in the night. He put his arms around her, and wrapped her in the garment of his great love, and took her through the pathway of the stars. She did not feel any cold nor pain, and he gave her a new, glorified body, so she could leave the poor old one behind."

"But she wouldn't have leaved me 'thout a word, when she loved me so, an' wanted me to go to heaven with her."

Dil's lip quivered, and her chest heaved with the effort of keeping back the tears.

"My dear child, there are many mysteries that one cannot wholly explain. Don't you remember telling me the Mission teacher said it was an allegory, a story that is like our daily lives? We are going heavenward in every right and tender and loving thing we do. We are the children of God as well as the children of mortal parents; God gives us the soul, the part of us that is to live forever. And when he calls this part of you to the heavenly mansions, he gives it the perfect new body. The old one is laid away in the ground. When Jesus was here he helped and cured people as I told you. But he does not come any more. He calls people to him, and sends his angels for them. So he said, 'It is very hard for poor little Bess to wait all winter, to suffer with the cold, the pain in her maimed body, to be afraid of her mother, to hear the babies cry when her head aches. She must come to the land of pure delight, and have her new body. She must be well and joyous and happy, so that she can run and greet her sister Dil when I send for her.'"

Dilsey Quinn was listening with rapt attention. But at the last words she cried out with tremulous eagerness,—

"Oh, will he send? Will he take me to Bess? You are quite sure?"

Her very breath seemed to hang on the answer.

"He will send. He has a place for you in the many mansions he went to prepare. And this little step we take from one world to the other is called the river of death, and you know how Christiana went through it. Sometimes the Lord Jesus lifts people quite over it."

There was a long silence. He could see she was studying the deep, puzzling points. The lines came in her forehead, white as a lily now, and her eyes seemed peering into fathomless depths.

Looking into the sweet, wasted face, holding the slim little hands, once so plump and brown, thinking of the heroic, loving life, he felt that indeed "of such was the kingdom of heaven."

"Well, 'f I c'n go to Bess," a sigh of heavenly resignation seemed to quiver through the frail body, "'n' I think the Lord couldn't help bein' good to Bess, she was so sweet 'n' patient; for 'twas so hard not to run about, 'n' have to be lifted, 'n' I couldn't always come on 'count of the babies 'n' mother 'n' things. 'N' she never got cross. 'N' I do b'lieve she understood 'bout Christiana, for after that she wanted so to go to heaven. An' she was so glad about her poor hurted legs bein' made well. We couldn't read fast, you know; an' we couldn't see into things, 'cause we hadn't been to school much. But she kinder picked it out, she was such a wise little thing, an' the pictures helped. But I don't understand 'bout the new body."

Her face was one thought of puzzled intensity.

"My dear little Dil, we none of us quite understand. It is a great mystery. The Lord Jesus came down from heaven and was born a little child that children might not be afraid of him, but learn to love him. When he grew to manhood he helped the needy, the suffering, and healed their illnesses. He went about doing good to everybody, and there were people who did not believe in him and treated him cruelly." How could he explain the great sacrifice to her comprehension? "Dil," he said in a low tone, "suppose you could have saved Bess great sorrow and suffering by dying for her, would you not have done it? Suppose that night the Lord Jesus had said to you, 'I can only take one of you to-night, which one shall it be?' What would you have done?"

"Oh, I'd let her gone. Was it that way?" The tears stood in her eyes, and her voice trembled with tenderest emotion.

"God loves us all as you loved Bess. But we do not all love him. We are not ready to do the things he tells us, to be truthful and honest and kindly. But he is ready to forgive us to the very last. And he knows what is best for us."

"Then that other body went to heaven," she said after a long silence. "An' I know now she must have been in some lovely place, 'cause that Sunday she come to me in Cent'l Park she was all smilin' an' strange an' sweet, an' beautiful like that picture you made. She looked jes' 's if she wanted to tell me somethin'. An' the Lord Jesus let her out of heaven 'cause I was so lost like 'n' uncertain."

The small face was illumined with joy. And to John Travis it was as the face of an angel.

He owed her so much. Again had God chosen the weak things of the world to confound the mighty. He thought of that other soul whose throes he had watched; whose guide-posts of science and philosophy had shed no light on the unknown hereafter; and how both of them had at last become little children in the faith. For when he promised to go to heaven with Bess and Dilsey Quinn, he meant to search out the way of truth if such a thing was possible. His had been a slower and more toilsome way, but Dil had seen and believed, and was among the blessed already. And he had come to a realization of the higher truths, not according to the lights of human knowledge, but faith in the Lord Jesus.

"I shall be so glad to see Bess. I'm most worn out an' wasted away longin' for her. But when I see her all straight an' strong an' lovely in heaven, I'll feel rested right away. I d'n' know how the Lord Jesus can care so much 'bout poor sick folks, when there's so many splendid people."

"Just as you cared for Bess."

"Oh, was that the way?" Her smile had the radiance of the everlasting knowledge. "But you see, I'd had Bess alwers an' loved her, 'n' he didn't know much about us, stowed away there in Barker's Court. So he's better 'n any folks. He had all that lovely heaven, an' he didn't need to come down. He must have loved people uncommon. It was like your stoppin' that day an' talkin' to us poor little mites. Why, 'twas jes' if you'd made a new splendid world for us!"

She stopped a moment and drew some long breaths. Then an eager light flashed across her face.

"Oh!" she cried, "I've found the lady who gev the wild roses to Patsey that day. She's here, 'n' all the children are jes' crazy 'bout her. An' she told me 'bout the picture you put me in. She said you'd be sure to come."

"She? Who?" John Travis was momentarily bewildered.

"Miss Deerin', Miss Virginia Deerin'. Ain't it a pretty name? An' she knows all 'bout that beautiful place of roses. I was hankerin' so for some, an' she went out to see 'f she could find any. I couldn't know you'd bring me such a lovely lot. Don't you know how Bess alwers b'l'eved you'd come, an' *she* b'l'eves jes' that way. An' she likes you so."

"Virginia Deering!" John Travis said under his breath, his whole frame athrill with subtle emotion, "what makes you think she likes me?" he asked softly.

"Oh, can't you tell it in any one's voice? An' their eyes get soft an' strange, 's if they were lookin' 'way off, an' saw the other one comin', jes' 's Bess come to me that day."

Then Dil raised a little and glanced out of the window, listened smilingly.

"She's come back. That's her voice. An' oh, won't she be glad to see you an' the heaps an' heaps of wild roses!"

150

XVI—ACROSS THE RIVER

Virginia Deering put by the children's clinging hands. Her mission had not been very successful. In one shady depth she had found a cluster of belated roses, their mates having blossomed and gone. But the children had enjoyed a rare pleasure.

She came up with a sort of reverent hesitation. She had been thinking of the journey "betwixt this and dawn," and trying with weak hands to push it farther and farther off, as we always do. Miss Mary had gone to the infirmary. The room was so still; then a soft, glad cry trembled on the air,—

"He's come, Miss Deerin'! An' oh, you won't mind, but he's been to that wild rose place, an' I think he's brought them *all* to me. Look, look!" and she stretched out her little hands.

Virginia paused, hesitated, her sweet face flushing and paling, as John Travis turned. He was not sure he had made up his mind to any certain step; but, having found her here, he was certain he should never let her go again in this mortal life.

Did it make any difference here in this sacred hour who had sinned? Could not even suffering love fold about another the garment of forgiveness? He took a step forward; she seemed to draw near by some inward volition, and stretched out her hands beseechingly. The sorrow and pain were ended. Was not love too sacred a thing to be bruised and wounded by trifles that should have been forgiven and forgotten as soon as uttered?

"Virginia," in a breathless sort of whisper. He stooped and kissed the quivering lips, and caught the tenderness of tear-blinded eyes.

"Little Dil, may *I* have Miss Deering's roses?" and he took them in his hand.

"I only found a few," in a faltering voice.

"But he's brought me hundreds. I'm most buried in roses. An', Miss Virginia, I told him you'd be so glad. An' it's all as you said, only I couldn't feel quite sure till *he* come. The Lord Jesus did take Bess to heaven that night; but he left me 'cause there was somethin' for me to do. It's all gettin' plain to me, only I ain't bright to see into things quick. But you can't both be mistook. An' now I'm all bright an' happy."

Did Virginia Deering say a year ago that she should always hate wild roses? She buried her face in them now, so that no one should see her tears. God had led this little human wild rose in the pathway of both. It had grown in the world's wilderness, and learned how to bloom out of its own generous heart. To her it was the lesson of her whole life.

Dilsey Quinn smiled. She knew nothing about love and lovers; but the atmosphere was sweet and cordial, and she felt that.

Virginia began to arrange some of the roses in a bowl, with the nervous desire of occupation.

"Please put thim here on the sill," pleaded Dilsey. "That's the way Bess had thim. An' I told him how you gev thim to Patsey."

John Travis gave a soft, quaint smile, and took a small case from an inside pocket. There were some poor little withered buds between the leaves. All the color had gone out of them, all the fragrance.

"You gave them to me," he said. "Do you remember? Bess had them in her hand."

Dilsey's eyes filled with tears. Virginia leaned over and looked at them, strangely moved. Then he laid the few she had gathered beside them.

"I'm jes' happy all through," Dil said with shining eyes.

Miss Mary came up with some broth.

"'Pears like I don't never want anythin' to eat again; but you're all so good. An' now I'm goin' to get well, though sometimes I want to see Bess so. An' I'd be sorry to go 'way from Patsey. Owen's gettin' to be such a nice boy. Patsey keeps him straight. I d'know who'd look after thim."

John Travis turned and gave her a rare, comforting smile. He owed her so much earthly and heavenly happiness; and he realized with a pang of anguish that she could never be repaid in this world. Had God noted the labor and love of this poor, unknown life, and written it in his Book,—the heroism so simply worked out, with no thought of self to mar any of it?

Miss Mary sent them down to supper.

"I am so thankful you had my letter in time," Virginia said softly. "We did not think then—"

She turned scarlet under his gaze.

"Your letter! Oh, *did* you write? My darling, thank you! You shame me with your trust, your sweet readiness to forgive. But I have hardly been at home these two days. I think," and his voice fell to a reverent inflection, "that God was watching over it all, and guiding our steps. It is a long story, and some day you shall hear it all, but in infinite pathos Dilsey Quinn's far exceeds it. Our whole lives will be more sacred to us for this remembrance. But I cannot bear to have her go. Is it as the nurse said?"

Virginia made a sign with her bowed head.

"I hoped so to give her a better, brighter life. I left a little work for her in the hands of a friend, and it came to naught. But perhaps—God's love *must* be wiser than our human plans, and his love is greater. We must rest content with that. But she has been an evangel to me."

Miss Mary bathed the face and hands of her invalid in some fragrant water. She had considered Dil a rather dull and uninteresting child at first; but her pitiful story that had come to light in fragments, her passionate love for her little "hurted" sister, and her wild dream of going to heaven, had moved them all immeasurably. The cheerful sweetness would have deceived any but practised eyes, and even now Dil seemed buoyed up by her delicious happiness.

"Won't they come back?" she asked presently, with a touch of longing in her voice.

"Yes, dear."

"I'd like him to stay."

"Yes, he shall stay."

The household had not been disturbed by the near approach of the awesome visitant. The children had not missed her, since she had brought no gayety to them, but rather grudged Miss Virginia to her. They were at their supper now. How easily they had forgotten the hardships of their lives!

Virginia and John Travis entered presently. The soft summer night fell about them, as they sat watching the frail little body, so wasted that its vitality was fast ebbing. She talked in quaint, disjointed snatches, piecing the year's story together with a pathos almost heart-breaking in its very simplicity. Her trust in him had been so perfect.

"I don't know what's 'come o' mother," she said, after one of the silences. "But Bess 'n' me'll tell the Lord Jesus 'bout her, 'n' mebbe he can do somethin' that'll keep her 'way from Mrs. MacBride's, 'cause she wasn't so bad before she took to goin' there. I've been so feared of her all the time, but I don't feel feared no more. Bess said we shouldn't when you came back, and wisht your name had been Mr. Greatheart. We liked him so. But they've all gone wrong in Barker's Court. Oh, can't some one set thim right an' straight, an' bring thim outen the trouble an' drinkin' an' beatin', an' show thim the way? It's jes' like thim folks leavin' the City of Destruction. An' oh, we've all come out of it, Owny an' little Dan. Maybe mother'll find the way."

"We'll find her and try to show her," said John Travis, with a voice full of emotion.

"Oh, will you?" There was a satisfying delight in her tone. "An' the boys? If some one'd look after thim, I think I'd like to go to Bess. Do you b'l'eve the Lord Jesus would come an' take me if I ast him? Seems so long since I had Bess."

"I think he will," Travis said, in a tone he tried to keep steady.

"I ain't pritty, like Bess, an' I can't sing."

"But you will sing there. And you will love the Saviour. That is all he asks."

"I can't seem to understand how he could be so good to poor folks. An' I don't see why they ain't all jes' wild to love Him. Tell me some more 'bout his comin' down from heaven to help thim."

With the little hand in his, he told the wider, greater story of the Saviour's love,—how he had come to redeem, to sanctify all future suffering in his own, to give himself a ransom. And even now Travis's mind reverted to the hours of discussion with his cousin. Ah, how could he have brought bread to that famishing soul, that had fed so long on the husks of the world's wisdom, but for the afternoon with the children, the meeting with the Lord Jesus in the way.

The moon came up and flooded the room with softened splendor, the summer night was fragrant with exquisite odors. Almost it seemed as if the very heavens were opened. The wide eyes were full of wordless rapture, and a great content shone in the ethereal face.

Then Dilsey moved about restlessly.

"My little Dil, what can I do for you?" he asked with tender solicitude.

A strange shudder seemed to run over her. Was it a premonition?

"I wish you'd take me in your strong arms 'n' hold me. 'Pears if I'd like to be clost to some one, just sheltered like. An' you an' Miss Virginia sing 'bout 'The rivers of delight.'"

John Travis lifted her up. She was so small and light; a child who was never to know any earthly joy or hope of girlhood, who would learn all the blessedness of life in the world to come. Virginia folded the soft blanket about her, and her face rested against the shoulder that would have been glad to bear a far heavier burthen for her. He took the cool little hands in his, and noted the fluttering, feeble pulse, the faint, irregular beating of the tired heart against his.

Sometimes both voices came to a pause through emotion. He remembered the other scene in the stuffy little room, and could see Bess's enraptured face.

Then Dilsey Quinn gave a little start, and raised her head, turning her eyes to him.

"I c'n understand it all now," she said joyously. "The Lord Jesus wanted me to wait till you come back, so I could tell Bess. An', Miss Virginia, she'll be so glad to know who gave the wild roses to Patsey. An' you promised her— you'd come. We was all goin' to heaven—together—"

The head dropped. The heart was still. The labor of the hands was done. The slow brain had the wisdom of the stars. But her eyes still kept the subtle glory; a radiance not of this world shone in her face as she left the night behind her and stepped into the dawn of everlasting life.

"She has seen Bess."

Then John Travis laid her reverently on the cot, and sprinkled a baptism of roses over her. The two left behind, clasped hands, their whole lives sanctified by the brave sweetness and devotion of this one gone up to God.

———————

No one told the "little mothers" that one of their number lay up-stairs in Miss Mary's room waxen white and still in her last sleep. They sang and played and ran and shouted, perhaps jangled as well. Death often met them in the byways of the slums, but in this land of enchantment they were not looking for it. Their holidays were brief enough; their days of toil and deprivation stretched out interminably. How could they sorrow for this pale, quiet little girl who had not even played with them?

In the afternoon John Travis brought up Patsey and Owen, who were stunned by the unlooked-for tidings. Dil had on her white frock, Patsey's gift, that had been both pride and pleasure to him.

Owen looked at her steadily and in great awe, winking hard to keep back the tears. Patsey wiped his away with his coat-sleeve.

"Ther' wasn't ever no girl like Dil Quinn," he said brokenly. "She was good as gold through and through. Nobody never loved any one as she loved Bess. Seems like she couldn't live a'thout her. O mister, do you think ther's railly a heaven as they preach 'bout? Fer if ther' is, Dilly Quinn an' Bess are angels, sure as sure. An' Owen, we've got to be tip top, jes' 's if she was watchin' us all the time. But it's norful to think she can't never come down home to us."

He leaned over and kissed the thin hands, and then sobbed aloud. But all his life long the tender remembrance followed him.

In a corner of the pretty burying-ground where they laid her, there is a simple marble shaft, with this quaint, old-fashioned inscription:—

"SACRED TO THE MEMORY OF

BESS AND DILSEY QUINN."

For, even if Bess is elsewhere in an unknown grave, her unfailing and sweetest remembrance is here with Dilsey.

And in one home in the city, made beautiful by love and earnest endeavor, and a wide, kindly charity that never wearies in the Master's work for the poor, the sinful, and the unthankful, there hangs a picture that Patsey Muldoon adores. It is Dilsey Quinn idealized, as happiness and health might have made her. The sunrise gleam in her eyes stirs one with indescribable emotion. She looks out so bravely sweet, so touched and informed by the most sacred of all knowledges. The high courage is illumined by the love that considered not itself; the tenderness seems to say, "to the uttermost," through pain and toil and discouragements; never quenched in the darkest of times, but, even when blown about by adverse winds, still lighting some soul. The face seems ripened to bloom and fragrance, and speaks of a heavenly ministry begun when the earthly was laid down.

And the old story comes true oftener than we think. Two put in the garden to keep and dress it, to watch over the little wild roses of adverse circumstances, crowded out of even the space and the sun needed to grow rightfully, out of the freshness and dew of happiness, yet making their way up from noisome environments, and struggling for the light and human care to fit them for the Garden of the Lord.

And these two, who go on their way in reunited love, understand the mystery of Dilsey Quinn's short life, and that the strange fine threads that connect us here are so many chords of the greater harmony of human love in its redemption. All their days will be hallowed by its tender remembrance, their work more fervent, their faith more enduring.

And thus it came to pass that the little bruised flowers of the slums lived not in vain.